# RISING
# STAR

**SYLV CHIANG**

Art by **CONNIE CHOI**

annick press
toronto + berkeley

Designed by Kong Njo

The author acknowledges the support of the Ontario Arts Council received through the
Recommender Grants for Writers program.

Annick Press Ltd.

We acknowledge the support of the Canada Council for the Arts and the Ontario Arts Council,
and the participation of the Government of Canada/la participation du gouvernement du Canada
for our publishing activities.

 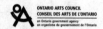

Library and Archives Canada Cataloguing in Publication

Title: Rising star / Sylv Chiang ; art by Connie Choi.
Names: Chiang, Sylv, author. | Choi, Connie, illustrator.
Description: Series statement: Cross ups ; 3
Identifiers: Canadiana (print) 20190068868 | Canadiana (ebook) 20190068884 | ISBN 9781773213118
    (softcover) | ISBN 9781773213125 (hardcover) | ISBN 9781773213156 (PDF) | ISBN 9781773213132
    (EPUB) | ISBN 9781773213149 (Kindle)
Classification: LCC PS8605.H522 R57 2019 | DDC jC813/.6—dc23

Published in the U.S.A. by Annick Press (U.S.) Ltd.
Distributed in Canada by University of Toronto Press.
Distributed in the U.S.A. by Publishers Group West.

Printed in Canada

annickpress.com
Follow Sylv Chiang on Twitter @SylvChiang
connie-choi.com

Also available as an e-book. Please visit annickpress.com/ebooks for more details.

MIX
Paper from
responsible sources
FSC® C004071
www.fsc.org

For my dad, who would totally drive
me to Comic Con if I asked him to,
and for my husband, who would
do the same for our girls.

—S.C.

# CHAPTER 1

"Finally!" From the sidewalk I see a small cardboard box sitting at my front door. I turn to high-five Cali, but she's already taking off.

I scramble up our steep porch steps behind her and use my house key to tear open the tape on the box. "Yes!" I hold up the advance copy of *Cross Ups V* in victory.

"C'mon, Jaden!" She grabs the key from my hand and opens my door. Even though her own front door is only a few feet away, we want to play together. And anyway, Cali's ArcadeStix controller is still at my place.

We drop our backpacks, jump out of our shoes, and run to the living room. Lights are all off, so I know I'm home first. I rip the plastic off and open the case. Instruction papers fall to the floor. Who needs those? I grab the disk and slide it in.

"It's beautiful," she says. We're staring at the picture on the cover as we wait for the start-up screen to appear on my TV. It shows all the characters around a giant roman numeral *V* because this is the fifth version of *Cross Ups*.

"Look at Kaigo!" I say. My main—a big muscly guy—has a new punk hairstyle and more badges on his kung-fu uniform. I wish I looked like him. I'm the scrawniest guy in grade eight. The only thing we kind of had in common was his old, messy hairstyle.

"Who's that?" Cali points to a girl with a long black ponytail that starts right above her forehead.

"Who cares? Let's go." I click through all kinds of pop-up screens, ignoring all the messages, until I can finally select the new Kaigo and start a match. "This is amazing." My thumbs tap the controller buttons excitedly. Ever since the announcement that *Cross Ups* was releasing a new game, it's been all I can think about. And the graphics totally live up to the hype. The new Kaigo looks so crisp.

We're battling in some kind of rainforest. That's new. And the colors are amazing. It's like one of those nature programs they show at Best Buy to make the TV look good. Everything looks so high def.

Cali's playing Ylva, the dire wolf–cross. She fits right in with this backdrop. Her cavewoman outfit is different too—shorter and striped.

In *Cross Ups*, the characters fight as people doing crazy hand-to-hand combat. They each have a bunch of Super moves they can use when they transform into the mythical creature they are crossed with. To transform your character, you have to wait for your Super Meter to be full, like mine is now. Kaigo is the dragon-cross, and I go for his Dragon Fire Super. It's his hardest Super, and I want to see what the new graphics look like. But Kaigo doesn't do anything. I'm so excited that I must have messed up.

Cali uses my mistake to grab me and spin me over her head.

The home phone rings. Yes, we still have a landline. My mom is stuck in the last century. She won't even let me have a cellphone.

"You gonna get that?" Cali asks, her onscreen-self pouncing on me as soon as I recover.

"Nah, it's just Devesh or Hugh calling to see if *Five* came. They've been calling every day since I told them about the advance copies." Cali and I are sponsored by ArcadeStix to play *Cross Ups*. Our rep, Kyle, sent us this advance copy of the new version so we can get our skills upped fast. He told us to keep it on the down-low because the game doesn't actually come out for two more weeks, but of course I told my friends.

"You should get that. Could be Hailey."

"And let you say you won the first match on *Five*? Nu-uh."

"So *Cross Ups Five* is more important than true love?" I know Cali's just going for the win, because she never teases me about Hailey.

"Shut up." I input Dragon Fire Super again, but Kaigo still doesn't transform into his dragon side and spin across the screen like he's supposed to. Okay, that's weird. I never miss that move anymore.

Cali's not having any problem with her Supers. She howls to transform into a canine beast and shoots shimmering moonbeams at me from her eyes. I crumple to the forest floor.

As soon as I'm out of hit-stun I go for my Dragon Tail Super. I burst out of my kung-fu uniform, mutating into my dragon-self and slashing my tail across the screen. Cali goes flying. That's better.

The phone stops ringing and the answering

machine—yes, we seriously still have one of those—picks up. After a few seconds, when the outgoing message must be playing, we hear: "Hi, Jaden. It's Kyle. Listen, a great opportunity has come up. Give me a call . . ."

I jump off the couch, sending my huge controller thumping to the carpet. My feet get tangled in the cord and I land on my knees. I lunge at the phone, knocking it to the ground. When I finally get it to my ear, I hear my screechy voice through the machine, "Kyle. I'm here."

Dead air on the other end.

"What do you think that was about?" I ask.

"Dunno. But I just kicked your butt."

I glance at the screen. A big K.O. announces my defeat.

This isn't the first time Cali's beaten me. But it still burns. On screen, Ylva celebrates, shaking her hands wildly above her head. Her win quote runs along the bottom:

STAND UP AND DEFEND YOURSELF!

Way to rub it in. I lay on the floor, wrapped in the controller cord, scrolling through the saved numbers on the phone, trying to find Kyle's.

Cali's phone buzzes on the table. "Hello?" She looks at me and mouths *Kyle*. After a few seconds she says, "Seriously?"

I bug my eyes out at her. "What's he saying?" I whisper.

She waves her hand to shake me off. After a long pause, she says, "Sounds amazing. I'll ask my mom and let you know." She hangs up and grabs her controller to start a match.

"So?" I practically scream.

"Oh, ArcadeStix wants to send me to Comic Con in New York." She tosses her long black hair over her shoulder, all casual.

"For real?"

"Yup. The makers of *Cross Ups* are launching *Five* there and they want me to demo it for the crowds. You know, get young gamers interested."

"Oh . . . But, he called me first."

"Yeah. Too bad you didn't get to the phone." She selects Ylva and waits for me to start the match.

"That's totally unfair. I was trying to call him. I've been on the team longer, I should get to—"

"Whoa, chill! I'm just messing with you. We're both invited."

"You serious?"

She nods. "They'll even pay for our flights."

"Awesome!" Flying to New York for Comic Con with my best friend? That's living the dream! I fall backward onto the couch and realize my thumbs are tapping like they always do when I'm stressed out. "That wasn't funny!"

"But they won't pay for chaperones. We'd go with Kyle."

I crash-land back in reality. Fly to another country with a guy we hardly know? There's no chance in hell my parents will go for that.

# CHAPTER 2

After Cali leaves, I spend hours playing *V*. The game is awesome. Tons of great new locations, and Kaigo's Supers look smoother and flashier. At least the ones I can do. Even after hours of practice, I still can't get Dragon Fire Super to work.

It's not the first time I've had this problem. I used to struggle with that Super back in the day, at my first tournament. But I learned to relax and not overthink the move, and then it came naturally. I roll my shoulders and force myself to take deep breaths. But it's not working. The more I think about relaxing, the more stressed out I get.

My mom makes me go to bed at eleven, but I can't sleep. All I can think about is Dragon Fire. I turn on the laptop in our room and search New York Comic Con. It looks amazing. I click *GUESTS* on the official website and what I see puts me in hit-stun.

Yuudai Sato, the most godlike *Cross Ups* player ever, is going to be there.

He won EVO, the biggest fighting-game competition in the world, twice. I watch his channel all the time. He's my biggest inspiration. Imagine meeting him? It would be the best moment of my life!

Once I'm sure my parents are asleep, I sneak down and put the game on training mode. Training mode! What am I, a newb? Dragon Fire Super is supposed to turn Kaigo into a whirling smoke storm that smashes through his opponent. I practice for, like, three hours but don't see a single smoke tornado.

It does feel like something is spinning in my stomach, though.

What if I can never get it to work? I won't be able to compete with *V* the way I did with *IV*. It's better if I don't go to Comic Con. Save myself the embarrassment of choking in front of a crowd and ruining ArcadeStix's reputation. It would be so lame to whiff Dragon Fire Super in front of my idol.

I fall into bed, defeated.

◄O►

"Dude, why didn't you call us?" Hugh whines when we meet up in the schoolyard the next morning.

Devesh joins in. "I wanted to stream your first *Five* match."

The guys love *Cross Ups*, but they aren't great at playing. Devesh streams my fights on Twitch. I never talk, but Devesh is a good commentator and gets a lot of views. And when Hugh joins in on mic, they get even more because Hugh just acts like a fool.

"You can't show us playing *Five* yet. Remember? No one's supposed to know we have it," Cali says.

"Who cares about *Five*?" Hugh says. "Comic Con in New York? That's amazeballs!"

"How do you even know about that?" I ask.

"ArcadeStix posted last night that you guys are invited. Everyone knows."

Ugh. Kyle keeps telling me to 'be more active on social media.' Kind of impossible without a phone. Last week there was an article in an online gamer magazine that called me and Cali "rising stars," and everyone knew before I did. "Well, it would be cool except . . ."

"I know, your mom." Hugh gets it. His dad is super-strict. But even he got a phone for his birthday this month. He pulls it out, takes off his glasses, and shows me the tweet from Kyle.

**ARCADESTIX** @ARCADESTIX SEPT 28
RISING STARS @JSTAR & @HERM1ONE INVITED
TO @NY_COMIC_CON TO SHOW THEIR MAD
SKILLS ON THE NEW #CROSSUPSV #FGC #ESPORTS

He wouldn't have written that if he saw me playing *V* yesterday.

"How are things with *your* mom?" Devesh asks Cali.

Her mom has MS. A few months ago her symptoms were so bad she fell and broke her leg. Cali had to move to Montreal to live with her dad and his girlfriend while her mom was in rehab. That didn't work out so good, since they had a new baby and everything. She lived with us for a while so she could start grade seven at Layton. Her mom finally came home last week.

"She's okay."

"Will she let you go?"

"I think so. She'll probably go with whatever Jaden's mom does."

"So, all we have to do is convince Jaden's mom to let him go. Easy. We've done that before," Devesh says.

To be honest, I never thought my mom would let me go to any video game event. She hates how violent *Cross Ups* is. So far I've been crazy lucky. I got to go to the Top Tiers Tournament here in town and the Underground Hype Tournament in Montreal. But Comic Con is in a whole other country.

"My mom's not going to let me go with Kyle—she hardly knows him. And a plane ticket to New York costs a lot of money. My parents aren't going to pay to take me."

The school bell rings and we head inside.

"You don't have to fly to New York," Devesh says. "You can drive there in one night. We went last March Break to visit my aunt. Me and my sisters slept the whole way."

I snort. "Like my mom's going to drive all night to go to Comic Con."

## CHAPTER 3

"Cali told me you guys got *Five* yesterday. What's it like?" Hailey asks during morning announcements.

Math is my first class of the day, and it's only bearable because I sit next to the coolest girl in school. She's sporty and smart. Plus she's got these freaky-cool, green-gray eyes that I have to stop myself from staring at. I didn't think she'd ever talk to me, but it turns out she's into *Cross Ups* and she has a lot of questions.

"It's good." I wish I was better at talking to her.

"What's different about it?"

"A lot." *Like the fact that I suck.* But I can't tell her that. What'll she think if she finds out I'm not good at *Cross Ups* anymore? It's probably the only thing she likes about me.

"Can I try it?" Hailey asks.

I answer before I can think. "Yeah. Wanna come over after school and play?"

It would be perfect, except Ty and Flash sit behind us.

"Oooh, Hailey, do you want to play with me?" Ty sings.

"Let's have a playdate," Flash adds.

"Shut up," I say.

"Make me," Ty answers. "We both know you can only fight in video games, *Rising Star*."

I didn't think they'd know about that article. Reading's not really their thing. My thumbs start tapping.

Hailey whips her head around so fast her curly ponytail grazes my cheek. "You wanna battle him?" she throws down.

Uh-oh! The way I was playing last night, I'm not sure I could beat them at *Cross Ups V*. And having a girl defend me is not going to shut these guys up. They're the kind of guys who think girls should stick to ballet and baking.

Fortunately, Mr. Efram walks by our desks with his stop-talking-and-listen-to-the-announcements look.

The voice over the speaker is wrapping up. "Finally, a reminder that tomorrow morning is the deadline to hand in nominations for student council elections. So far we have one set of candidates for class president and vice president. If no other nominations are received by the deadline, the positions will be acclaimed without an election. Exercise your democratic right to run for office!"

Behind us Ty and Flash give each other high fives.

"Seriously?" Hailey says, shaking her head. "Those two *cannot* run our school. That settles it. I'm getting a nomination form today." Hailey is one of those people who joins everything. She's in the

photography club, the band, the eco club, and on every sports team. She even writes for the school paper. She's my exact opposite.

Mr. Efram starts the lesson. "Let's imagine we're in the DC universe. You're Batman, or Batgirl, and you get this message from the Riddler." He unfolds a piece of chart paper. "Riddle me this—"

Ty calls out, "If I'm Batman, I'm getting Alfred to solve math problems for me."

"Superheroes don't cheat, Tyrell," Mr. Efram says.

That shuts him up. Last year, Mr. Efram caught Ty and Flash copying off me, Devesh, and Hugh, and the consequences sucked for all of us.

While we work on the riddle, my invitation to Hailey hangs in the air, like an unclaimed coin in *Super Mario Bros.* I'm so tired from playing *V* all night. Hailey does most of the thinking and writing.

Finally, when we're almost done, she says, "I can't come over today. I've got tryouts."

"Liar." Ty coughs out the word.

I look at him.

"It's *football* tryouts after school." Flash smiles. "Girls' basketball is tomorrow. I guess she doesn't want to *play* with you, Rising Star."

These guys can't do math, but I believe they've got the tryout schedule memorized. They're on all the teams. Flash even got his nickname because he's the fastest guy in our grade. The only person he can't legit beat is Hailey.

My face feels as red as Kaigo's flames. Why'd I even ask her to come over? I should've just offered to lend her the game.

She glares at them. "Actually, touch football is coed. Coach Lee said he wants me on the team for sure."

That shuts them up.

Then she turns to me. "You trying out?"

I don't even blame Ty and Flash for laughing. I suck so bad at sports. Hailey should know that from summer camp. Unless maybe I tricked her with those sweet passes I threw her way. But in a real game, I'd get sacked before I ever had the chance to release the ball.

"Uh . . . can't. Gotta practice *Five*." This is true. If I don't get my Dragon Fire Super back, I'm going to get kicked off ArcadeStix—the only team I've ever been on.

# CHAPTER 4

Hugh and Devesh follow me and Cali home after school.

"You actually asked Hailey to come over?" Devesh says, holding his fist out for a bump.

"She really wants to try the game," I say, ignoring his fist.

"Or she wants an excuse to hang out with you," Devesh says, pushing his fist back at me. "Because she knows you're friends with me."

Hugh snorts.

"Even if she did, she's on so many teams and clubs, I don't think she's got a free hour in her week," I say. "Plus now she's going to run for class president."

"There's going to be an election after all? I figured the two losers who brought in their forms were going to win by default," Devesh says. "Who wants all that work?"

"Those two losers are Ty and Flash," I say.

"No! They can't add, and they're going to run our school?" Even Cali, who's a grade seven newbie at Layton, knows Ty and Flash's reputation.

"Hopefully everyone will vote for Hailey now instead," I say.

"Who's her running mate?" Hugh asks.

"Her what?" I ask.

"You have to run as a team of two: a president and a vice president," Hugh explains. "Haven't you been listening to the announcements?"

Why would I listen to the announcements? It's all about teams and clubs. Nothing that matters to me.

It's a good thing Hailey didn't agree to come over, and not just because of how awkward my friends are. I still can't get Dragon Fire Super to work, and it's totally messing up my game. I mean, I beat Hugh and Devesh, but they're just messing around, playing each character, one by one, to try them out.

"I like the new Blaze," Hugh says about the phoenix-cross. "He's more muscly."

"Muscles are useless if you can't get him to do

any moves. I like the new Saki," Devesh says, playing the yeti-cross. "He's faster."

He only thinks that because he's doing better against me than usual. I'm so tired. Plus I'm freaking out so much I'm starting to miss my other Supers too.

Cali notices. "What's going on?" she asks after she wins the third game in a row. "You're playing like crap today."

I yawn. "I didn't sleep much." But that's not it. It's like my connection to Kaigo is gone. He used to feel like a part of me. Now, he's a stranger.

"What time are your parents coming home?" Devesh asks.

Even though I'm tired, my spidey-senses tingle. Devesh is up to something. I look at Hugh and he puts the bag of Doritos down. He senses it too.

"Look at me, Dev," I say.

He turns his head my way.

"No, seriously. Look at me."

He turns his whole body to face me and puts his chin on his fist, wrinkling his monobrow. "What up, bro?"

"This is important. When my mom gets home, do *not* say anything about Comic Con."

"What? Why? Your mom likes me. I totally convinced her to let us go to Montreal, didn't I?"

Hugh laughs. "Um, no."

"I had to do a lot of damage control after you opened your big mouth," I say.

"Did we go to Montreal or not?" Devesh says.

I roll my eyes.

"If we wait for *you* to do something, we'll be waiting forever."

"Please," I say.

He puts his hands up like he's under arrest. "Fine, I promise not to say anything to your mom about Comic Con."

Thank god. Truth is, I'm not even going to ask her. I'll just tell everyone she said no. That way I have an excuse not to go and I won't end up looking like a loser. I mean, I'm supposed to be a "rising star," but I can't even do Kaigo's best Super. I can't let people see that.

The front door opens, but it's not Mom. It's my dad and my brother, Josh. They're both wearing sweats, which means they're coming from a practice for one of Josh's teams. What sport does he play on Thursdays? My brother's the MVP on all his teams, and my dad coaches some of them. Ty and Flash would fit better in this family than I do.

"That the new game?" Josh asks, plunking down on the couch next to me.

"Get out of here. You stink!" I push him, but it's like trying to move Kaigo—he doesn't budge. A lot of people don't realize we're brothers, because we look so different. Then they say I look like Mom, and he looks like Dad. I don't like being compared to a little Chinese woman.

"Let's play. You beat me, I take a shower."

Josh is the one who taught me how to play *Cross Ups*, and how to hide my gaming from Mom. She actually used to be even more strict than she is now. We weren't allowed to play any violent games or watch violent movies. She thinks animated Disney movies are violent. So, all the blood flying around in *Cross Ups* makes her cringe.

I don't want Josh beating me. The way I'm playing, he probably can. "The advance copy is just for me and Cali."

"Whatever. You let Devesh and Hugh play."

The guys suddenly act real interested in the last chips in the bag.

"Aw, let your brother try," Dad says. "He needs to lose at something. Scored three goals today. One off a header. Talk about getting a big head."

Right. Thursday is soccer.

"Fine. Play Cali." I shove my controller on his lap and head to the kitchen for a new bag of chips.

"So, Mr. Stiles, you coach a lot of Josh's teams, right?" Devesh says.

"Sure do. This guy keeps me busy. And keeps me in shape." I bet Dad's patting his stomach.

"You go to a lot of tournaments out of town?" Devesh asks.

"For sure," Dad says. "This summer we went to three. Ottawa, Niagara. Even Chicago."

"It's a good thing Jaden's not into sports. You wouldn't have time to take him to tournaments too," Devesh says.

"Oh, I'd make time," Dad says. "That's what parents do."

My spidey-senses are doing more than tingling now. They're trembling on high alert. I fly back into the living room just as Devesh goes all-in.

"So, you could take Jaden to New York for Comic Con?"

# CHAPTER 5

Dad turns and looks at me. "You want to go to Comic Con?"

"It's just that Kyle invited me and Cali to demo *Cross Ups Five* there," I say, opening the bag of salt and vinegar, all casual. I'm annoyed Devesh asked him, but it's not like he's going to take me.

Dad smiles like he just found out I got drafted by the New York Yankees. "That's incredible. When?"

"Next weekend," I say. "Don't worry, I know you're too busy."

Devesh gives me a what-the-hell look over my dad's shoulder, and then calls out, "It's a long weekend."

"Is it? Josh, do we have anything?"

Josh shrugs.

Dad pulls out his phone. Is he actually considering this? "Titans don't have a tournament." That's the soccer team. "Lightning practice on Saturday is optional." That's Josh's hockey team. "Tryouts for basketball start the Wednesday after . . . You know what? I'm in. Let's do this!"

I choke on the chips. The vinegar burns in my nose. Hugh claps me on the back until I'm done my coughing fit. Then he gives me a huge bro hug.

My mind races. This isn't how it was supposed to go. I throw out a desperate, "What will Mom say?"

Devesh looks ready to punch me in the face.

"Mom?" Dad shrugs. "I'll talk to her."

Dad calls Kyle to get the details, and then calls Cali's mom to make sure she can go. Cali beams when he nods to her.

Then, Dad gets really into planning the road trip. "Good thing ArcadeStix reserved the hotel already. I wanted to get a second room, but everything's booked up." It's like he's been waiting for so long for me to be good at some sport, and he knows this is as close as I'll ever get.

"You are so lucky," Hugh says.

I don't respond.

"What's the matter?" Devesh says. "You in shock? Is your mind blown?"

Oh, my mind is blown, all right. I should be so hyped. My dad just agreed to take me and my best friend to Comic Con, where Yuudai Sato is going to be. But instead, I'm freaking out.

Why does Devesh always have to jump in and take over? He ruined my plan. Again.

Now I have no excuse not to go. My secret will be out. Everyone will find out I suck at *V*. And Dad's just going to end up disappointed.

Devesh is all smiles. "See? Leave it to me and your dreams come true."

Of course, *my* dreams aren't enough for Devesh. He looks over my dad's shoulder while he checks

out the venue online. "You know, Mr. Stiles, I have an aunt who lives in Weehawken," he says in his talking-to-adults voice. He turns his phone to my dad, showing him a map. "Technically it's in New Jersey, but it's only a short ferry ride to Manhattan— Google says eighteen minutes to Javits Center, where Comic Con is."

Devesh's parents each have a ton of brothers and sisters, and they take a lot of road trips to visit his aunts and uncles in random places in Canada and the United States. When we went to Montreal this summer, Hugh and Devesh stayed with one of Devesh's uncles.

Devesh goes on. "We'd love to come along and support Jaden and Cali. If you'd be kind enough to let me and Hugh drive down with you guys, we could stay with my aunt. We wouldn't be any trouble."

He elbows Hugh, who looks like he just got called in to kick a field goal after sitting the whole season on the bench. "Oh, yeah. That would be so awesome, Mr. Stiles. We'd be eternally grateful."

"Sure, why not. We'll make this a real boys' trip."

Cali clears her throat.

"Sorry, Cali. You know what I mean." He winks

at her. "You're like one of my boys. Hey, Josh should come too."

Seriously? It's not enough that I'm totally going to disappoint my dad and fail in front of my idol. Now my all-star brother's going to be there to rub it in my face.

Obviously, I have to stay up all night practicing again. I don't totally suck. My Dragon Breath Super is solid, and burning everything up in a giant, fiery wind feels good. Plus, I can do a lot of damage flailing my massive tail around, since my Dragon Tail Super hits every time. But I still haven't pulled off a single Dragon Fire Super.

I'm still winning, but that's in training mode. I'll have no chance playing against good players at Comic Con without it.

Is my controller broken? I put in *Cross Ups IV* and try Dragon Fire. Kaigo spins into smoky destruction. No problem. Switch back to *Cross Ups V* and nothing.

This is a mega problem. They want me, the "rising star," to demo *Cross Ups V*, live, in front of thousands of people, and I can't do Kaigo's best

Super? Plus, even more people will watch me fail online. Me. The guy who totally freaks out when he has to do a presentation in front of the class. My head is spinning like I'm being juggled by Ylva.

Why can't I get this? It's like the input has changed to some secret combination. My usual strategy—looking online for tips—won't help because the game hasn't even been released yet.

My thumbs tap uncontrollably and my T-shirt is damp. I'm sweating like I've actually been doing all the moves myself. I've versed every single character in *Cross Ups V*, even the new ones.

I wonder if Cali can do Kaigo's Super in *V*. I've kind of been hogging the game, to be honest. Maybe I could ask her tomorrow. I don't want to admit I can't do it, but I'm desperate. I wonder, could I do Ylva's Supers?

I try. It takes me a while, but I manage. The Moon Howl Super doesn't hit every time, but Wolf Tail and Wolf Claw are easy. Not smooth like when Cali does them, but I can get them all to work.

I scroll through the character list. There's a reason I main Kaigo: I love everything about him—or at least I used to. He's the best character, at least from *Cross Ups IV*. But there are some new ones in *V*.

First up is Aatom, a basilisk-cross. I can get him to Super, but he's basically a giant snake. I don't like snake-crosses. Even though they're strong, they're slow. Kaigo has power *and* speed.

Next, I try Turan, the girl from the cover with the ponytail coming out above her forehead. It turns into a horn when she Supers, which is lame. *Cross Ups* already has a unicorn-cross, Lerus. But at least all the Supers are easy to play. And Turan's way stronger and faster than Lerus. I look at her player sheet and she's actually some weird Chinese creature called a luduan. When it turns out she executes my bread-and-butter combo, the one I go to all the time, exactly like Kaigo, I'm sold. I train with her until I can't keep my eyes open anymore. When I fall into bed it's almost 5 a.m.

◄o►

A pillow to the head barely wakes me.

"Get up, geek!"

I force an eye open and register the sun coming through the window, and Josh, fully dressed. I try to open the other eye, but sleep pulls me back.

I hear my sister calling down the stairs. "Jaden's still in bed, Cali."

Crap. Cali and I walk to school together. We usually leave way before Josh and Melanie. The twins go to a high school that starts half an hour later than Layton. If they're leaving, I'm super-late. I moan.

"Wha!?!" That's Mom's voice. "Still in bed?"

I'm up like Kaigo recovering from a hit. I don't need my mom finding out why I'm so tired. "I'll be ready in, like, two minutes," I yell down the stairs.

I throw on the jeans I wore yesterday, then dig through the clean laundry basket in the hall until I find a black T-shirt. I grab a piece of gum from the pack on Josh's trophy shelf and scramble down the stairs, pulling the shirt over my head. No time to fix my hair, but it's always standing up in crazy directions—no one will notice.

"You need breakfast," Mom says in Mandarin as I breeze through the kitchen, grabbing the last bagged lunch sitting on the counter.

"Not hungry," I say.

"At least take a banana," she calls.

I grab my backpack off the hook, jump into my sneakers, and fly out the door, calling, "No time" over my shoulder.

"Took you long enough." Cali jumps off the swing

that sits on her side of our shared porch and follows me down the steps. "Hey, wait up!"

As we warp-speed it, I tell her about my night playing Turan.

"Finally you try a girl character."

"C'mon. I'm not like that. I know girls can win. And Turan is amazing."

School's in sight now and kids are still outside, so, miraculously, we haven't missed the bell. Cali stops and gives me a once-over. "I guess that explains the T-shirt."

"What?" I look down at my black shirt and see the sun reflecting off something. Are those silver sparkles? "What the? No!"

Cali giggles. "So, you didn't mean to wear that?"

"Argh! Must be Melanie's. What's it say?"

"You don't want to know."

"Yes, I do." I scrunch my chin to my chest and try to read the glittering, fancy script from upside-down.

Cali whispers, "Girls Rule."

# CHAPTER 6

Of course, today of all days, Hailey's waiting by my locker. I'm wearing my backpack in front to cover the sparkly words.

"There you are," she says, her green-gray eyes twinkling. "I have a plan to beat Ty and Flash, and I need your help."

"Yeah, sure, anything," I say. I probably sound like a total loser, but I really would do anything for her. Plus, I need her to go away so I can deal with my wardrobe malfunction.

"Remember I told you yesterday how I'm going to run for president?"

I nod.

"Well, I need a running mate for vice president, and we nominated you." She says this like it's a good thing.

"We?" I ask. That's when I notice Devesh and Hugh standing behind Hailey.

"I don't think so," I say. "I mean, I'll totally help you. Put up posters and . . . hand out buttons or . . . whatever. But I'm *really* not a good candidate," I stammer.

"I disagree. In fact, you're the perfect candidate. Since that article came out, everyone at school knows your name. And name recognition is a huge part of any campaign." Did I mention Hailey's on the debate team?

She pulls out a piece of paper with a list of signatures running down it. "We got the twenty signatures we need on your nomination form this morning, no problem. People know you."

"Cali was in that article too. I nominate her."

Cali freezes like she's in hit-stun. I feel bad, but I have to save myself.

"You have to be in grade eight to run," Hailey says.

Cali sticks out her tongue. She's only a month younger than me, but since my birthday is in December and hers is in January, we're in different grades. Lucky her.

I shoot Kaigo's flames at Hugh and Devesh. Their names are on that list. What are they thinking? They know I'm not a leader.

I turn back to Hailey and stammer more. "You don't know me . . . I can't . . . there's no way I can give a speech . . ." I'd rather take a real-life infinite attack than get up in front of the whole school and talk. The idea makes me want to hurl. I turn to Devesh and Hugh. "C'mon guys, help me out."

Devesh clearly does not understand what I mean by help. "I'll write your speech for you. Just make lots of promises and then throw candy into the crowd."

"We need you, J," Hugh says. "If you don't try, Ty and Flash automatically rule Layton, and this year will totally suck. Hailey's right, people know your name—they'll vote for you."

Hailey pleads, "I'll do all the talking today. The real speech isn't for two weeks. Please say yes. I can't run without a VP and the form is due to Madame Frechette before the assembly."

The bell rings.

"When's the assembly?"

"Now."

Every instinct is telling me to say no. But how can I disappoint the girl of my dreams in her moment of need? It's like Leia in that scene from *Star Wars*. *Help me, Obi Wan Kenobi, you're my only hope.* Too bad she sees me as Obi Wan, when really I want to be her Han Solo.

◄○►

The next ten minutes are a blur. Hugh and Devesh disappear to their homerooms for attendance. I ransack my bag and my locker at hyper speed, trying to find my gym shirt. Must have left it at home in my rush. Mr. Efram refuses to let me bring my backpack to the gym for the assembly. Then, he won't let me go to the washroom, where I was planning to hide out. It's like he's Professor X and he can read my mind.

Madame Frechette, who's in charge of student council and is also the school French teacher, opens the assembly, saying something about a last-minute nomination, and the next thing I know me, Hailey, Ty, and Flash are standing on the stage.

I keep my arms crossed, but my skinny biceps don't cover all the writing. Sparkles float around my head, like when Kaigo's in hit-stun, and I take a few steps back so I won't fall off the stage. Then I realize they're coming from the stage lights bouncing off the glitter.

Ty and Flash talk first. Everything they say is about Layton's sports teams. New uniforms, entering more tournaments, a high-tech score board for the gym. Then Flash starts beatboxing and Ty lays down a full-on rap:

*We're Ty and Flash and we're way, way cool.*
*Layton will be the bomb when we're running*
*this school.*
*Basketball, volleyball, soccer, and hockey.*
*This year watch how we win every trophy.*
*We promise you can ride on the new team bus.*
*All you gotta do is vote for us.*

They drop their mics, leaving behind a high-pitched squeal as they prance off the stage.

Hailey bends over to pick up the microphones. Not sure why she's handing me one. I take it awkwardly, trying to keep my shirt covered. A strange thumping sound fills the gym until she leans over and clicks my mic off to dull the sound of my thumbs tapping wildly against it.

"We have a dream for Jack Layton Senior Public School and we want to share it with you all today," she begins. Her voice is strong and confident, yet soothing, like waves lapping at the shore. I start to feel a bit calmer. I just wish she wasn't using the word *we* so much. "We believe every student is equally important. We're all cool in our own way. This year, let's celebrate everything, not just the sports teams and clubs, but all of our fun times. All the moments that make school special."

She's totally got this. Kids are looking into her amazing eyes like they're being hypnotized. She speaks a bit louder now, like bigger waves rolling in. "If you think school is boring, think again. We're going to make this an awesome year—full of fun memories."

Her voice amps up, like waves crashing to shore. "One day, when you're old, you're going to look back on your years at this school. Me and Jaden want to make sure you all have the best memories of these days. *Every* one of you. Vote Hailey and Jaden for a memorable year."

How the heck did she come up with that in less than twenty-four hours?

Madame Frechette looks at me like I'm supposed to say something. I shake my head, and the room starts to spin again. She's not getting the hint, and the pause is so long I can't take it anymore. I need to get off this stage.

"Uh, what she said," I say, pointing to Hailey.

Everyone laughs. I don't know if it's because I sound like an idiot after her Barack Obama–style speech or if it's because of the sparkly *Girls Rule* I uncovered when I pointed at her. My palms get really sweaty, and the laughter sounds farther and farther away. And then I do an unplanned mic drop of my own and everything goes dark.

# CHAPTER 7

I'm lying on the bench in the office with an ice pack under my neck. Hailey's sitting on the floor next to me.

"Told you I'm not a good candidate."

"The good thing is, everyone will remember us."

This girl is too much. I fainted on stage in front of the whole school wearing a *Girls Rule* T-shirt. That's not something I want everyone to remember. The only good thing I can see is, at least the most embarrassing moment of my life is over.

Then I remember Comic Con, and my palms get moist again. It's going to be way worse when everyone, including Yuudai Sato, finds out how bad I am at *Cross Ups V*.

Madame Frechette, who was kind enough to signal the stage crew to close the curtains while I was lying on the stage, says, "Did you have breakfast

41

this morning, Jaden? Sometimes low blood sugar can cause people to faint."

"Um . . . no," I admit. But I know this wasn't a blood sugar issue. This was a freaking-out issue.

"Is anyone home? Do you want us to see if someone can pick you up?"

"No," I say, fast. "My parents are at work." The last thing I need is my mom finding out about this. But I do like the idea of going home. "I can just walk."

"I'm not comfortable sending you home on your own. Why don't you eat something and see how you feel? Hailey, can you stay with him this period?"

Great. Now she's babysitting me. We walk to my locker and I take out the lunch I grabbed from the counter this morning. *Please don't be anything weird.*

"We should talk campaign strategy," she says, like we still have a chance to win this election. "We only have ten days before the vote."

"You sure you still want to do this?" I ask, unwrapping a sandwich. Tuna. Great. Fish breath.

"Of course." Her pretty eyes go all serious. "We have to. We're the only ones who can stop Ty and Flash from turning this school into an NFL training camp. People are counting on us to make this year awesome."

"I think they're counting on *you*," I say.

"Hey, we're a team." I like the sound of that. "And plus, any guy who has the confidence to wear that T-shirt is freaking cool. I'd vote for you." I like the sound of that even more. She smiles. "Now, let's make the most of this free period you scored us."

◄○►

The next morning is Saturday. When Devesh and Hugh knock on my door before nine o'clock, I know they're serious about this campaign. Usually nothing gets Devesh up before noon on a weekend.

My kitchen is campaign headquarters. Luckily my mom is working at the diner and my dad and Josh are at a tournament, as usual.

"Even with your 'fall' yesterday, you can totally win this," Devesh says, making air quotes around the word *fall*.

"How you figure?"

"Um, you've got Hailey on your side," Hugh says. "You heard her speech. It was dope."

We both squint at Hugh. *Dope* isn't a word he normally uses.

"Plus, you're practically famous," Devesh continues. "That article about you and Cali was huge. And now Comic Con is listing you guys on their website as guests. That's huge too. You know who else is listed as a guest?"

I shrug. I've seen the list, but thinking about it freaks me out.

"Yuudai Sato, three Avengers actors, Dwayne Johnson." He points his phone at me. "You are on the same list as superheroes and The Rock. You can do this."

"C'mon. You know me. I'm not cool."

"The good thing is, no one else knows you," Devesh says.

Ouch. That hurts like a fireball to the head.

Hugh notices my pain. "Dude, people know your name. But hardly anyone knows what you're like."

"So, basically you're saying I don't have a lot of friends. How is that good?"

Devesh says, "You have a mysterious quality. People hear your name and wonder, 'Why don't I know him? Because he's shy or because he's too cool to talk to me?' So we make them think it's the second one. You just have to fake it till you make it."

"Pretty sure I can't fake cool. Plus, I have to make a speech in front of the whole school next week. I definitely can't fake that."

"Sure you can. I'll write it for you," Devesh says. "I'll make it real short. Keep the mystery alive and keep you on your feet."

"I only said three words yesterday. Can you make it shorter than that?"

"That's because you weren't ready. You can do this, J. We'll help you practice on the way to Comic Con," Hugh says.

Wish I believed it like they do. Or are they just faking it too?

Hailey arrives with her friend, Tanaka, and all kinds of poster board and paints. Cali comes to help too.

"Don't you dare post that!" Hailey's talking about the video of me fainting that Devesh is showing everyone on his phone. He's got it on a boomerang loop so it runs back and forth. I fall down and pop back up, over and over.

"Um . . . we already did. Like six different versions. The best is him falling in slow-mo while Alicia Keys sings 'f-a-a-a-a-a-a-a-a-a-a-a-a-a-a-all.'" Devesh fails at singing the line, but we still all recognize the song. "It got tons of likes."

"Personally, my fav is the one where we put the cat face app on him and played the song 'Memories.' It goes with the theme of your campaign," Hugh says.

"Our theme is *cats*?" I am so confused.

Hugh explains. "No, your theme is *memories*. But the song is from a musical called *Cats*."

"You guys are weird," Hailey says. "I like you, but stop posting those."

"First of all, too late. It's already out there." Devesh holds up his fingers as he counts. "Second of all, you said name recognition is huge in elections, and everyone is talking about Jaden now. And third of all, if he acts ashamed of it, Ty and Flash will see his weakness and use it against him."

My *weakness*? As if I only have one?

"Plus, it's hilarious," Hugh says. "Look how his eyes roll back before he goes down."

While they work out their creative differences, I put my head on the table. What have I gotten myself into? I don't have time for this. I should be practicing *Cross Ups V*. There's only one week before Comic Con. One week! I'm not even close to ready. When

Ty and Flash see me crash and burn there, they're going to add that to my list of weaknesses.

"I agree with Hailey. No point embarrassing Jaden," Tanaka says. "It's cool how you stepped up to save the school from those jerks."

"So cool," Hailey says.

I keep my head down so no one can see how red my cheeks are.

"So, we're agreed. No more posting the video." Hailey speaks with such authority that even though Hugh and Devesh haven't actually agreed, I know they'll follow her orders. "We need to start talking up all the reasons me and Jaden would be good leaders."

Easy for her. She's so perfect, it's like she invented perfect. People will do anything for her. All she has to do is turn those eyes in their direction. That's how I got into this whole mess.

But me? The only thing I'm really good at is staying under the radar. That's the opposite of being a leader. But it's not easy. I work hard to blend in so I'm not a target for jerks like Ty and Flash. Being a candidate in this election is like standing in the middle of a huge bull's-eye in the cafeteria with a sign that says *Free Shots*.

I hear a familiar laugh. "Jaden a leader? You're joking, right?" I look up to see Melanie, still in pajamas, yawning. She's scanning the election signs that Tanaka and Cali have started painting on the kitchen table. One says, "Jaden for Vice Pr—"

Everyone fills her in. Devesh even shows her the video. This is bad. Melanie does not need this kind of ammunition.

She takes Devesh's phone and pushes her fingers across the screen to magnify the image. Then she starts laughing. "Are you wearing my shirt?"

## CHAPTER 8

My kitchen morphs into the set of one of those cooking-contest shows, except instead of meals, everyone is making posters. Devesh argues for a while, but eventually even he accepts that Hailey is the head chef. Since I suck at art, and everyone laughs at my attempt to draw bubble letters, no one cares when I leave to play some *Cross Ups V.* People drift in and out of the living room to take breaks from painting and play a few rounds against me.

They're all interested in Turan, and the more I play her, the more I like her. So I come up with a plan for Comic Con. I'll play Turan instead of Kaigo. I'll just act like I want to show off a new character. No one will expect me to be as good with Turan as I am with Kaigo, since she's brand new. And playing a girl character might even make me look good. But I'm not wearing that *Girls Rule* T-shirt again.

Hailey's so dedicated to the election campaign that she's the last one to take a break. She flops on the couch next to me and picks up the small black controller. She smells good. Is that orange? Or peach?

"This is so cool. You get to play the new *Cross Ups* before anyone else."

I nod. *Ugh, say something, Jaden.* "Yup. It's cool."

"Who's that?"

"Turan." Why is that all I say? It's like my tongue gets big and awkward in my mouth when she's close to me.

"What's she like?"

"She's perfect." *Like you.* Geez. *Get it together, Jaden.*

"You like her better than Kaigo? Because you're awesome at Kaigo."

She just called me *awesome.* And she's called me *cool* twice in the last two days. Why can't I act awesome and cool? "Yeah, I really like her. A lot." Ugh. It sounds like I have a crush on Turan. Say something less stupid. "Wanna try my controller?" *Better.*

"Totally. But just for a few minutes. Then I have to get back to work." She doesn't mention that I'm literally doing nothing to help. After yesterday, she's probably just glad I didn't quit.

I pass the huge red ArcadeStix controller to her. It's my prized possession. I don't let anyone use it.

"So, you going to main a girl now?" she asks, selecting Ylva.

I do my best to sound awesome and cool. "I want a change. I've been playing Kaigo forever." Then I have a horrible thought. "You're not making *Girls Rule* our slogan, are you?"

She laughs. "Nah. I wouldn't change things up without talking to you. I told you, we're a team. We'll stick with *Making Memories*, if that's okay with you."

This is a memory I won't forget. I'm actually having a real conversation with Hailey.

"Stop letting me win," she says.

"Uh . . ." I am playing pretty bad. But it's because I'm distracted by the fact that *the* Hailey Williams is sitting next to me on my living room couch. And she smells so good. *Focus, Jaden.* "I just wanted to give you a chance to try out the game."

"It's no fun if I know you're not even trying."

I step up my game. On screen I grab her and throw her down hard. It's so weird to be beating up Hailey. My Mind Control Super shoots shock waves out of my horn, paralyzing her.

"Hey, I can't move. What kind of creature is Turan, anyway?" Hailey says.

"She's a luduan. Some mythical Chinese unicorn-deer thing. She can do this too." I pull back on the stick and press three buttons at once. Turan rears up, jumps in the air, then disappears for the count of three. Ylva convulses on the screen.

"Are you serious? She can go invisible?"

A few more moves like that and Hailey's K.O.

"You're godlike," she says, passing me back my controller.

"You too," I say before I can stop myself.

"Whatever. You could beat me with one hand."

"I mean, at the election thing." I drum the buttons on my lap while I talk. "Your speech was amazing. You'd be a godlike class president. I hope I don't lose this for you."

"Don't put yourself down. I think you're actually going to win this for us."

That's when I have a crazy thought. What if we do win? So far, I've just been going along for the ride. I mean, I really want Hailey to win. But what if I actually end up vice president of the school?

◄○►

Just as I'm getting hungry, the doorbell rings and the smell of pizza wafts into the house. This is how organized Hailey is. She got everyone to pitch in and placed the order. She could totally run the school. She could probably do the principal's job.

They've cleared the kitchen table of paint and posters. Things look so clean. Did she mop the floor? I don't even know where my parents keep the mop.

"Check these out," Hailey says, pointing to all the signs leaning against the walls and cupboards to dry.

Some of the posters have pictures from *Cross Ups* with slogans like:

**Let Jaden be your champion—He's got the moves!**

**Jaden will fight for you like he does in *Cross Ups*!**

Oh man. It's a good thing people don't know how I fight in *Cross Ups V*.

Other posters just say **Making Memories** with big, blank spaces. "What's with these?" I ask.

"I'm going to fill them with pictures that look like memorable moments," Devesh says.

"Isn't that a great idea?" Looks like Hailey and Devesh have come to a truce. "Now let's talk about another important part of our campaign—election promises."

Hugh grabs two slices of pepperoni and says, "Dudes, no more French class. Video game class instead." He takes a bite, but holds up his finger while he chews so we know he's not done. "And cola from the drinking fountains."

Hailey sighs. "We're not going to promise things we can't deliver."

"Then you don't know anything about politics," Devesh says, reaching into the box. "You'll never win if you don't lie."

"Promising a memorable year is good," Cali says.

"Thanks. But people are going to want to know more details," Hailey says. "Any ideas?"

Hugh won't give up. "No homework would give us more time to make memories."

Devesh gives him a fist bump. "So would a shorter school day."

"Not happening," Hailey says.

"I'd remember candy pencils." Hugh snickers until he catches Hailey's glare.

"How about a yearbook?" Cali says.

"Ooh, I like that," Tanaka says, grabbing a can of pop from across the table. "We could totally do that."

"Layton used to have a yearbook," Devesh says. "My sisters have them."

"Yeah, so do Mel and Josh." I take a bite, and cheese stretches like Spiderman's webs between the slice and my mouth.

"That's weird. Why didn't we have one last year?" Hugh reaches for a third slice.

"Maybe it's too old-school," Devesh says.

"What do you think, Jaden?" Hailey asks. "Should we promise to make a yearbook for all the memories?"

The only memory I want to make this year is to not look like a fool in front of Yuudai Sato and everyone else at Comic Con. "I guess . . ." She looks like she's expecting something better than that. All

I can think to add is the obvious: "People have to wait a long time for a yearbook."

Hailey hasn't even taken a slice yet. She's all business. "Good point. A yearbook doesn't come out until the end of the year. People want something now."

"Like the video we posted of Jaden," Devesh says. "That was instant."

"Stop with the video already," Tanaka says.

"Wait." Hailey's deep in thought. "He's right."

Don't tell me we're back to that. "You said we're not gonna post that anymore."

"Not *that* video," Hailey says. "What about videos of cool things happening around the school? We can show people that this year is already on its way to being memorable."

Devesh swallows. "I could put that together. Anyone can share their videos. We can do one every week."

"Won't that be a lot of work?" Cali asks, lifting a glass of water to her mouth.

"Yeah. But it'll be fun too," Devesh says. "I'm going to be a director one day, so it'll be good practice. And Hugh will help."

"I will?" Hugh asks.

"We can show the videos at assemblies," Tanaka says.

"And at the end of the year, we'll have a whole bunch of them. Like episodes of a TV show," Devesh says.

"We can call it *Layton: Season One*." Cali spreads her hands out like she's revealing a magic trick.

Hailey's eyes sparkle at me. "What do you think?"

I have to admit, "Sounds cool."

"I can see it now," Devesh says. "Episode one will open with Jaden's epic fall."

Sigh.

# CHAPTER 9

"Did you see this?" After everyone leaves, me and Cali are chilling on the couch. She passes me her phone. She's got the Comic Con site open to the blog.

### YOUNG GAMERS FROM ACROSS
### CONTINENT TO SHOWCASE
### *CROSS UPS V* IN U-18 TOURNEY

At the bottom it lists the names of the players competing. Mine and Cali's jump out at me.

Under-eighteen tournament? "I thought we were just playing for fun."

"Looks like they changed things up."

Aw crap. My plan is falling apart. I was just going to demo Turan and show what a cool character she is. But I can't compete with her. Not at that level. Not yet.

"Did you see the prize?"

I look back down.

*The winner will play Yuudai Sato in a live-streamed match.*

"Whoa!" I'm excited just to see Yuudai Sato in person. Maybe get to speak to him. Even if I suck at Comic Con, I could say I met Yuudai Sato. If I'm totally lucky, maybe he'll even sign my controller. But to actually battle him? That's crazy—like, in-my-dreams crazy.

I have to win this. And if we were playing *Cross Ups IV* I bet I could too. But on *V*, I've got no chance.

━◦━

"Did you know Jaden's running for VP of student council?" Melanie narcs as soon as she sits down at the dinner table.

My parents stare at me like a luduan horn is growing from my forehead. I'm kind of insulted. No one would be surprised if Josh or Melanie were running for student council.

Josh reaches over my bowl for the black bean chicken and says, "Good luck," in a voice that means I've got no chance.

"What made you decide to do that?" Dad asks in a trying-too-hard-to-be-casual tone.

I stab my chopsticks into my rice. "I didn't decide." When they keep staring at me, I add, "My friends are making me do it," and shovel rice into my mouth.

"Why?" Mom asks, worry oozing from her eyes.

I shrug, happy my mom doesn't let us talk with our mouth full.

Melanie says, "His running mate is a pretty girl."

They all nod, like that makes a lot more sense.

"That's not why." My whine doesn't convince anyone.

Dad pours himself a drink and tries to rescue me by changing the subject. "I'm really looking forward to our boys' trip." He keeps calling it that.

"You sure everything is planned?" Mom asks.

"Yup. We leave after school Friday. I've even scheduled a dinner stop at White Castle for burgers."

Josh gives him a high five. I've never heard of the place, but I guess they've eaten there on their sports trips.

"But what about safety? Did you plan a meeting spot? New York is a dangerous city. And do you all remember our family password?"

"Ugh, Ma, we're too old for that," Josh says.

"Your brother and Cali are only twelve," she says, like we're babies. "What if one of them gets lost? How will they find you?"

"Cali has a phone, so she'll be okay," I say. "If you loved me more, you'd get me one too. I mean, if you ever want to see me again."

Melanie snorts. "Nice try, loser. We had to wait until high school to get phones. So do you."

"Don't worry so much, Linda," Dad says. "I'll leave with five kids and bring back five kids. Maybe not the same ones I leave with, but—"

"Steven!" Mom's stare shuts him up.

"Relax. It'll be fine. Hey"—he changes the subject—"Josh got MVP." He doesn't say the word *again,* but it's hanging in the air all around that sentence.

"Good job, Josh," Mom says. "We are very proud of you."

Josh smiles, then turns to me. "I heard there's a kids' tournament at Comic Con. Maybe you'll finally win, Jaden."

"Not with Cali there," Melanie says.

"Jaden does very well," Mom says. Nobody else backs her up, and I think of all Kaigo's missed Supers.

I flash back to last year when the grade-seven gym teacher, Coach Lee, saw my name on the attendance list.

"Stiles? Are you Melanie and Josh's little brother? Can't wait to work with another Stiles." Josh was on every boys' team during his years at Layton. And Melanie was on a lot of the girls' teams too. Plus, they did the newspaper and debate team. Basically, they're more like Hailey than me. Coach Lee's excitement didn't last long. By the end of the first class I could tell I'd be lucky to get a C.

The twins are a lot to live up to. Sometimes I wish I was an only child.

Monday morning at school, Devesh punches me in the shoulder, smiling like a crazy jack-o'-lantern. "Guess what I did!"

I shrug. With Devesh, it's hard to even imagine. He does things I'd never think of, like putting his sisters' fake nails on the cat.

"Oooh, let me guess." Hugh pushes between us. "Did you actually do your homework?"

"No." Devesh snorts.

"I know. You drew sad-face emojis on Ty and Flash's posters."

"No," he says, glancing at the photoshopped pics of our rivals made to look like they're juggling balls for every sport. "But now that you mention it, those balls really are calling out to be emojied."

"Right?" Hugh says.

"Give up?" Devesh asks.

Hugh tries one more time. "Did you ask that new girl for her phone number?"

"There's a new girl?" But we all know Devesh is not-so-secretly in love with Cali.

"Just tell us," I say.

"I ordered costumes!"

I look at Hugh, then back at Devesh. "Isn't it a bit early for Halloween?"

"First of all, it's never too early for Halloween," Devesh says. "And second of all, we're going to Comic Con. Hello? Cosplay."

Hugh turns to me. "What's he talking about?"

"Cosplay," Devesh says again, like repeating the word will make us understand. "Tell me you guys know about cosplay. At comic conventions, dressing up is huuuge."

"So you ordered three costumes? Isn't that expensive?" Hugh asks.

"My mom's cousin runs an online costume store in India. Actually, I got one for everyone, including Cali, Josh, and your dad."

Hugh laughs. But I can totally see my dad wearing a costume. He loves Halloween. When I was in grade four, me and Dad actually made our own droid costumes using cardboard boxes and other random things we found in the garage. He was C-3PO and I was R2-D2. I remember we got gold spray paint on mom's car and she was mad. Dad even had plans to make Josh a Stormtrooper costume, but Josh wasn't interested. He was in grade eight, like I am now.

The bell rings for class. "Hold on. What costumes did you get?" Hugh asks.

Suddenly, I have visions of skin-tight Lycra superhero costumes, or a two-person unicorn. I'm *not* walking around with my head on Hugh's butt. "I don't think I'm allowed to cosplay," I say. "I have to wear my ArcadeStix T-shirt."

Hugh glares at me.

"It'll be fine," Devesh says. "In fact, it's going to be epic!"

That's what I'm afraid of.

# CHAPTER 10

Ty and Flash's posters are everywhere, but so are ours.

Each one has a blown-up picture of me and Hailey doing something "memorable." There are pictures of us climbing a mountain, dressed up for prom, eating ice cream sundaes, even on paddleboards. Devesh found some great bodies to stick our heads on. We look awesome. I do a double take of the one where we're playing video games and realize it's really us in my living room.

With my face on every wall of the school, even with a different body, my cover is blown. I can't walk down the halls without being recognized. People keep coming up and talking to me. They're asking questions about our campaign promises. Sometimes I say, "Ask Hailey." But sometimes I try Devesh's fake-it-till-you-make-it idea. I imagine the kind of guy who'd run for VP, the guy from the posters, and say the things that guy would say. Like, when Justin complained to me that his bike was stolen, I said, "We're totally going to talk to the principal about getting the bike racks moved to the front of the school so they can be under video surveillance. If we win. So, vote Jaden and Hailey." When I hear myself talk like that, I think I might actually have a chance.

Fortunately, we don't have to do anything else until Election Day, which is exactly seven days away. That's when we'll make our big speeches. Then it's the vote. Thank god we don't have to do a debate like they do in high school. That would mean a lot more talking in front of a crowd. Plus, it's hard to argue with Ty and Flash because what they say doesn't make a lot of sense.

Ty wants to debate though. Any chance he gets, he tries to start an argument with me. In the halls. In the cafeteria. And especially in math class.

"Hey, Rising Star," he whispers during Mr. Efram's algebra lesson.

Hailey shushes him.

"I said Rising Star, not Hailstorm."

So, he's figured out Hailey's gamertag. Looks

like he's been doing some research. That's a first. He usually doesn't put effort into anything besides sports. Why does he care so much about this election?

When I don't turn around, he just talks to my back.

"I hear you've got another big tournament this weekend. Guess you won't have time to practice your speech. Hope you don't faint again." He's found my biggest weakness. I guess I gave him that one.

"Our speech is going to be a touchdown," he continues. "We've got choreography and backup singers."

"Sounds more like a half-time show," I snap.

Mr. Efram looks over. "What's that, JStar?" Ever since he found out I'm a gamer, Mr. Efram calls me by my gamertag.

"Sorry, sir." I'm still a bit in character as the guy who's running for VP. That must be why I keep going. I talk math to make it sound like I was listening the whole time. "I was just surprised you solved for $x$. I would have solved for $y$ first."

"And you likened that to a half-time show?"

Hailey's giggles encourage me. "Math gets me real excited."

I glance to the side. Hailey's green-gray eyes sparkle to reward my boldness. She presses her lips together to keep her laugh in.

"Uh-huh." Mr. Efram's not buying it. "Since this is so exciting for you, by all means, come on up and solve for *y*. Maybe the class will be moved to cheer you on."

I get up and do the equation. Math's my best class. I can solve algebra equations like I play *Cross Ups*. *Cross Ups IV*, that is.

When I get back to my seat, Hailey leans over and whispers, "You're so smart."

Man, now she thinks I'm a geeky gamer *and* a math nerd.

"Oh my god, look at the old gym uniforms," Cali says. She's pointing at an old yearbook in front of her.

We're in the library with Hailey and Tanaka and stacks of old yearbooks. It was Hailey's idea to go through the old albums to research our memory theme.

"What are we looking for, exactly?" I ask.

"We need to find out what kinds of things make

the best memories. What stands out? What's everyone talking about?"

I grab the most recent yearbook. It's from four years ago, when Josh and Melanie were in grade eight.

I flip to the grad photos and find the last names starting with *S*. There they are. Joshua Stiles and Melanie Stiles, side by side. It's funny to see them at the exact age I am now. I was hoping they'd look geeky, like me. But even though they look younger, they're still obviously cool kids. It's something about the way they look into the camera—like they know they're not losers.

I flip through pages of sports teams. Almost every picture has one of my siblings in it.

Hailey leans over. "Is that the last book?"

"Yup."

"Stop," she says when I get to a picture of the yearbook committee. She points to the teacher in the photo. I've never seen her before. "That must be why they stopped doing a yearbook." She reads the name under the photo. "Mrs. Kumahara doesn't work here anymore. I guess no teacher took it over when she left."

I keep flipping pages until I find the student council. Madame Frechette is standing with a group of students in front of the big red Layton school crest on the wall in the gym.

"Who were the president and VP?" Tanaka asks.

"I bet they were your brother and sister," Cali says.

"Nah. Mel and Josh could never stop fighting long enough to work together. Plus, they were both too busy with sports teams and clubs," I say.

"That's not stopping Hailey," Tanaka says.

I read under the photo. "President: Lannister Eklund—hey, that's Lanny Eklund, Ty's brother. He was on Josh's hockey team last year." I used to have to sit through all their games until Mom finally agreed I could stay home alone.

"No way," Tanaka says. "Is he as big of a jerk as his brother?"

"I dunno. He's a good body checker, though."

"Sounds about right," Hailey says.

I flip back to the sports teams and see Lanny in all the same pictures as Josh.

"So, Ty's just like his brother," Cali says. "On all the sports teams at Layton, playing rep hockey, and now running for president."

"Actually, Ty didn't make the rep team," Hailey says.

"He didn't?" How does she know that? Don't tell me she's on the boys' rep hockey team too.

"No. The guys were talking about it at football tryouts. Flash made it but Ty and this other guy didn't."

That must suck for Ty. Trying out for teams your brother made and getting cut is hard. That's why I gave up a long time ago.

# CHAPTER 11

Friday after school, Dad, Josh, me, and Cali pack up the minivan.

Mom hands us containers of grapes and cut-up apples. "Eat them before you get to the border. They won't let you take fruit into the United States."

I'm pretty sure she's just saying that so we'll eat the healthy snacks.

Dad's got the van in reverse, but Mom's still talking to him through the window. "Call me when you get there. Make sure the kids eat enough. Don't forget to have a meeting spot." As we turn off the driveway, almost as an afterthought, she calls, "Have fun!"

When we get to Hugh's building, he wedges his bag into the cargo area behind the third row of seats. Josh is in the passenger seat. Me and Cali claimed the middle, so he squishes past us into the third row and we roll out.

"Oh geez," my dad says when he sees Devesh standing on his porch with a backpack and a huge hockey bag. He rolls down the window. "What is all that?"

"Cosplay! You're going to love it, Mr. Stiles."

My dad turns to look at me.

"He wants us all to dress up," I explain.

Devesh corrects me. "We *are* all going to dress up."

"I don't think so. That bag's not going to fit in there," Josh says.

Hugh and Devesh survey the cargo area. With our five bags, there's hardly room for Devesh's backpack. Cali gets out and folds down her seat so Devesh can shove the hockey bag onto the back seat. It takes up two out of the three spots.

"You're going to have to leave that here," my dad says.

"No! I've been planning this all week."

"Fine. We'll take the costumes," Dad says. "But you'll have to stay here. Your choice."

Devesh looks like he's about to cry.

I take bags from the back and give them to people to hold on their lap or put under their feet. Devesh wedges the hockey bag into the cargo area and, after three tries, forces the back door closed. Then he wedges himself into the last seat.

"Are you finally going to tell us what the costumes are?" I ask.

"Not yet. When you see them, I want it to be a moment you'll always remember."

The drive is long. It probably feels longer because my dad insists that the driver gets to pick the music. His radio station plays All Eighties, All the Time.

"I brought your speech." Devesh pulls a crumpled paper out of the backpack on his lap.

"Great," I sneer. I flashback to the stage and my fingers start tapping.

"Dude, we can help you memorize it," Hugh says.

Cali smiles. "C'mon. Read it."

I sigh and look down at the paper.

A few seconds later she says, "Out loud, loser."

Dad and Josh are singing along to a super-whiny song, so it's only my three friends listening. "Fine. I'm Jaden Stiles and I want your vote. You—"

Hugh cuts me off. "Seriously, dude? Are you a droid?"

"Put some expression in your voice," Devesh says. "Say it like that guy on the radio."

The song ended and a DJ is talking now. His smooth, deep voice rolls like music over the words.

It feels so fake. "You might know me as a pro-player for ArcadeStix. I play *Cross Ups*, and I plan to cross things up here at Layton! Hold for applause—"

"Don't say that part," Devesh says.

I continue in my DJ voice. "I know about making incredible memories. This weekend I met my idol, the beast, Yuudai Sato. Then I won a tournament so I could battle him, and I won that too. It was a moment I will never forget." I turn to Devesh. "What the?"

"You will. Keep reading."

"We can help you make memories just as good. Vote Hailey and Jaden for a memorable year! Throw candy into the crowd."

"Yes! Candy!" Hugh high-fives Devesh.

"What d'ya think?" Devesh asks.

Hugh considers. "I say go with chocolate bars because lollipop sticks could hurt someone."

"I mean the speech, moron. Short and sweet, right?"

It is short. Not even half a page. Maybe I can do this.

"You've got lots of time," Cali says. "Say it again. More expression this time."

⸻◦⸺

After about a hundred run-throughs we're across the border and we're starving. Dad pulls over at a rest stop where we get some burgers and fries. Then, one by one, everyone in the back falls asleep. Devesh is first, then Hugh and Cali. I listen to my dad and Josh talking about soccer and laughing about some guy who always misses his shot when it comes to penalties.

"He hasn't made one all season. Why do you keep picking him?" Josh says.

"He needs it." Dad pauses. "It's not all about the game we're playing that day. You've got to build stronger players to make the team stronger. You'll see. One day he's going to get one in. Then he'll be on fire."

"But the more he misses, the lower his confidence gets," Josh says.

I know how that guy feels. It's like me with the Dragon Fire Super. Are they going to laugh at me?

"Every time I pick him, he knows I believe in him. That's an important message."

"I don't know, Dad . . ."

I'm so tired my eyes are falling shut. Next thing I know I'm standing on a soccer field. But I'm not wearing soccer gear; I'm dressed in a kung-fu uniform like Kaigo's. I look over to the side of the pitch, and my dad is signaling to someone to get on the field. It's Cantu, the hydra-cross from *Cross Ups*. I move closer and jab at her. She's solid and doesn't notice my punches. I kick too, but I might as well be kicking a wall. I jump up for a Dragon Fire Super but nothing happens. I just land back on the ground.

Cantu's neck divides into multiple heads. But they're not her normal snake heads. Each one has Josh's face on it.

"I won MVP," says one.

"I scored the winning goal again," says the next.

"You can't even Super," says another.

My dad's on the sidelines calling, "Go for it! C'mon, you can beat him," but I can't tell if he's talking to me or Josh.

I throw fireballs, but Josh back dashes across the field at supersonic speed. Now he's got a ball and he's heading for the goal. I'm the goalie. The ball bounces off my shoulder.

Or is that even a ball? Someone's punching me.

"C'mon, loser," Josh says. "Wake up."

# CHAPTER 12

I'm the only one left in the car. I see Cali's shape holding her bag and yawning in the dimly lit parking lot. Josh is standing at the door. "Get out of the car, dork."

"C'mon, Jaden," Dad says. "We just need to check in and then you can go back to sleep."

I pull my jacket closed against the chill of the night air.

"Where are the guys?" I ask.

"Devesh and Hugh?" Josh says. "We dropped them off twenty minutes ago. Didn't you notice when they crawled over you to get out?"

The bright lights and busy energy of the hotel lobby wake me more. We slump into big comfy chairs grouped around a coffee table while Dad lines up at the front desk.

"What time is it?" I ask.

Cali checks her phone. "One thirty."

"Why are so many people still up?"

"They call New York the city that never sleeps," a voice says. I turn to see a pretty girl with heavy brown bangs sitting in the fourth chair. She squints at me, then looks at Cali. "Oh my god. Are you those gamer kids from Canada?"

Now I'm awake.

"Yeah . . . ," Cali says. "We're from Canada."

"I knew it. I looked you guys up. Herm1one, right? Oops, I mean Cali. And you're Jaden, or JStar, right? I follow you on Twitch. That's so cool we're staying at the same place—"

"Um, who are you?" Josh interrupts.

"OMG are you their rep? You probably think I'm, like, a stalker. It's not like that. I'm part of the *Cross Ups Five* launch too. I'm Hena." She sticks her hand out to Josh, who shakes it hesitantly. Before he can answer her question, she turns back to Cali. "You're the only other girl in the U-18 competition. I looked everyone up. Not just you guys. But I remember you guys because you're the youngest by, like, three years. The next youngest are all like fifteen. I'm sixteen. I'm so excited to be here. My mom's just checking us in. Our flight was delayed and I'm so tired."

This is her tired? Her words are like an infinite attack on my tired brain.

"I bet everyone will go nuts when they meet you guys. You're like celebs. I watched that video of you, Jaden, from T3, where you played Kn1ght_Rage. It has like three hundred views. But that's an amazing story that a lot of people would be interested in. I could make that go viral. Can I interview you for my Twitch channel some time?"

"Uh, sure."

She pulls out her phone. "Can I take a selfie with you? It can be a teaser for our interview."

This is too weird. She holds her cellphone out and leans in to put her face next to mine. Wonder if she can feel the heat coming off my cheek. Should I smile? Probably best to just act cool. I look into the camera like I'm a saying *'sup?*

"Thanks," she says.

Dad comes over. "All set," he says.

"See you tomorrow," Hena says.

We grab our things and head to the elevator.

"Who was that?" Dad asks.

"That," Josh says, "is Jaden's first fan."

◄o►

I fall into bed and I'm out in seconds. When I wake up, I wonder if that conversation with Hena actually happened. Did I dream it?

I haven't stayed in a lot of hotels. Only when we went to Florida for a vacation, and when we went to Aunt Janie's wedding in Sault Ste. Marie. This room is tiny compared to those. There are two beds, one against each wall, with a small space between them. I'm hanging out of the bed me and Josh shared. No idea how we both slept in this narrow thing.

We're all on top of each other as we try to get ready. The rollaway bed Cali slept on blocks half the bathroom door until Dad folds it up and shoves it into the hall.

I pull on my red ArcadeStix shirt. Cali's wearing hers too. We're here to represent. I don't see the huge bag, so I guess my dad made Hugh and Devesh take the costumes with them when he let them out in New Jersey. When I see what my dad's got on, I wish he'd wear a costume instead.

"Ugh, Dad, is that seriously what you're wearing?" I say.

"What? This is my cool gamer shirt." He bought the *GDLK* shirt at my first tournament because he thought it meant Good Luck. Now that he knows it stands for godlike he uses the word all the time when he wears it.

Cali smiles. "It's okay, Mr. Stiles. It's cool."

"You mean it's *godlike*?" he asks.

"Uh, sure," she says and shoves her toothbrush in her mouth.

We grab a few things from the hotel buffet, but I'm not hungry. I'm freaking out. What will Kyle think when I play Turan instead of Kaigo? What will the world think?

We walk to the Javits Center, where Comic Con is taking place. I have to remind myself we're actually in New York City. It looks a lot like downtown Toronto, except for all the aliens and superheroes walking around. Devesh wasn't kidding about cosplay. We don't need directions or a map—we just follow all the people in crazy costumes.

There are Zeldas, Pikachus, Ghostbusters, and a lot of Avengers. And there are tons of costumes I don't recognize. I think people just invent their own characters. Some look like manga characters, some look medieval, and pointy elf ears are everywhere.

"I feel like we're on the set of some weird *Lord of the Rings* cross-over movie," Josh says.

"Everyone looks so godlike," Dad says. We all roll our eyes.

We follow the crowd into a huge lobby that has windows for walls and ceiling. Even though the doors to Comic Con won't open for another fifteen minutes, it's packed. We find Kyle near the ticket booths.

"Cali, Jaden, how are you?" he says, giving us each a fist bump. Then he shakes my dad's hand. "Hi, Mr. Stiles. And this must be your older son. You guys look so much alike." No one ever says that about Dad and me.

"Josh," Josh says, shaking Kyle's hand too.

"Welcome." Kyle hands us each an entry badge on a lanyard.

"Um, why does it say speaker on my badge?" I ask, panicking.

"There's no gamer category," Kyle explains. "Speaker is for anyone presenting on a stage. Since you guys will be on the stage for the tournament, that's your category. The rest of your entourage just gets the regular weekend pass. There are two more there for your friends. Luckily, a couple of the older players didn't need their free parent passes. Last-minute passes are impossible to get."

A loud sound, like a chair dragging across a floor, makes us all turn. It's a wookie, carrying a very real-looking bowcaster. This place is nuts.

"Never seen a game launch like this before. You guys should be real proud to be invited. You're the only Canadian players here."

Great. So we're not just representing ArcadeStix, we're representing the whole country. No pressure.

# CHAPTER 13

We shuffle over to make room for a fairy and her photographer who are setting up a full-on photo shoot by the window. They even have those weird umbrella things to reflect the light.

"So what's the plan for today?" Dad asks.

"Well, Jaden and Cali have a get-together now for all the U-18s who are here for the launch. You're welcome to come along," Kyle says.

"When's the tournament?" Dad asks.

Kyle pulls out a program and leafs through it. "At two o'clock the designers are showing the trailer for *Cross Ups Five* on the main stage. They'll do a big intro and hype up the crowd. The tournament is right after that."

"All right. Why don't you guys go hang with the cool kids for a bit and we'll meet up for lunch. Back here at twelve thirty?" Dad says. "We'll check out some panels."

"Here's the schedule," Kyle says. "You'll want to line up at least an hour before doors open for any panels. They fill up fast."

Dad and Josh look at each other and shake their heads. "Maybe we'll just check out the exhibit hall," Dad says.

When the doors open, me and Cali follow Kyle through a maze of Star Wars and Star Trek characters. The costumes are amazing. One guy is wearing full-on Optimus Prime gear. He's being lead around by two friends because his costume is so big he can hardly see out of his windshield.

At the end of the hall, a door says:

**CROSS UPS V: U-18—PRIVATE FUNCTION**

There's a poster promoting *Cross Ups V* on the door, and my name is on it. Along with Cali's and the names of all the other U-18 players.

I can't believe this. I'm a VIP at Comic Con!

Kyle opens the door to reveal even bigger *Cross Ups V* posters and cutouts of the characters that people can pose with for pics. I look at Cali and smile.

"Check it out," she whispers, pointing to the back wall where consoles are set up, tournament-style.

And in the middle of the room—a table with donuts. Nice! Wait till I tell Hugh and Devesh about this. They're going to freak.

"This is Jaden and Cali," Kyle announces to the guy in a staff shirt taking names at the door. "And I'm Kyle. We're from ArcadeStix in Canada."

Only two other guys are here so far. They look a lot older than us. I'm glad my dad and Josh didn't come.

"Canada? Cool," says the guy with jagged black hair and smudgy eyes. Is that makeup? He's wearing a black hat with a brim and a dent in the top. He looks like one of the K-pop stars on Melanie's bedroom wall.

I look at Cali. She doesn't get as nervous around new people as I do. "Where you from?" she asks.

"Here." He doesn't offer his name. I notice a nametag on his band T-shirt, but it's partly covered by a black vest. All I can read is the start: Ga—

"Lucky," she says.

"How long was your flight from Canada?" the other guy asks, running his hand through spikey brown hair. A Nintendo shirt hangs off his thin shoulders. He looks familiar, but I've never heard of the name on his tag. LEANDROS. How do you say that?

"Oh, actually—"

"We drove," I say, cutting Cali off. I feel bad, but I need to talk too or people will think I'm a loser.

"You drove all the way here from Canada? I'm from Alexandria and I flew." I have no idea where that is and my face must show it. "It's just outside D.C.," he adds.

"Right," I say. He must mean Washington, D.C. Not that I could find it on a map.

"Could have taken the bus. But if people want to pay for my plane ticket, I'm taking it," Leandros adds.

"Nintendo paid your flight?" Cali asks, pointing to his T-shirt.

"What? No." He waves a dismissive hand. "I'm not sponsored. Too restrictive. I told people on Twitch about my invitation to come here and asked for donations."

That's where I know him from. I've watched his Twitch stream before. He's hilarious, the way he makes fun of the people he's playing. His name is something else online though. Termin8? Must be his gamertag.

A loud revving noise from the hall gets everyone's attention, and we stare out the door at a guy with a chainsaw attached to his arm like a hand. It takes me a second to realize the chainsaw isn't moving—it's a prop—and the noise is coming from a speaker inside it.

"Can you believe all these people in costumes?" Leandros says.

I'm about to say how cool they are when Eyeliner Guy laughs. "Yeah, I know, right? Cosplay is so lame."

So, I guess his makeup isn't part of a costume. Does he always wear that?

"Real gamers would never, right?" Leandros says.

"Never," I say. Cali looks at me and I give her a tiny head shake. She'd better not say anything about our costumes or we'll look like losers. I promise myself not to wear whatever Devesh brought.

Cali changes the subject. "So, who do you guys main?" She sounds so casual. I need to be like that too. No one here knows me. It's like Devesh said—if I act like I'm cool, they'll believe it.

Eyeliner Guy says, "Blaze. You play Ylva, right?"

Cali looks surprised. "Yeah," she says.

Leandros says, "Everyone's heard about you two. *Rising Stars.* That's hype. Cali, right? Gamertag Herm1one?"

She nods and bumps his outstretched fist.

He points to his name tag. "Leandros." It sounds like lee-*ann*-dros. He turns to me. "You're Jaden, right?"

I nod.

"JStar. You play Kaigo, like me."

We fist bump, then I remember. "Well, I used to."

The guy from New York heads over to the table and grabs a donut. The rest of us follow. As he raises his cruller to his mouth, the vest moves and I read the rest of his name. Gabe. We munch while we talk. I tell them I main Turan now, and they raise their eyebrows.

"Why'd you switch?" Leandros asks.

I feel my thumbs start drumming against my leg. I can't give the real answer: desperation. "I was looking for a challenge."

"Risky, right before a tournament," Gabe says, shaking his head. He's looking at me like I'm so cool. *Me.*

"You sure you're twelve?" Leandros says.

"I think it's important to have more than one character in your arsenal," I say, with swagger that surprises me.

It surprises Cali too, and she looks at me weird. Now that I think of it, she's been telling me for a while that I should play more than one character. But these guys don't know that. They see me as a rising star in the *Cross Ups* world.

Just like *Cross Ups V* is the new, improved *Cross Ups* game, I've got to be a new, improved Jaden. A cooler version of myself.

That's Jaden V.

# CHAPTER 14

More players stream into the room. In the end there are sixteen of us under-eighteens and a bunch of adults. It's hard to tell if they're sponsors or parents.

Hena was right. Everyone has heard of us and they all want to talk to us. It's like we're celebs. A lot of them read the "Rising Stars" article. After talking to all those kids at school about the election, this is easy. These guys aren't asking tough questions. They just want to talk *Cross Ups*.

Jin from Jersey asks, "Which character do you hate versing?"

I tell him I can't stand Ylva. "She's so jumpy—always in the air—it drives me crazy."

He agrees with me.

Lee from Houston wants to know, "You seen Yuudai Sato yet? What do you think he's like? I couldn't find any interviews with him online. He's mysterious."

"Yeah, totally mysterious," I say. Devesh said people think I'm mysterious too. Cool.

Weston from Miami says, "*Five* definitely rules over *Four*. I love how the graphics are way better, but they kept the game play the same. Don't you find it so easy to transition?"

I nod. No way I'm telling anyone about my trouble with Dragon Fire Super in the new game. As far as these guys know, I'm godlike.

Besides Cali, the only other girl in the room is Hena. She starts talking to Cali right away and never stops. Not even to breathe. Her thick bangs almost cover her eyes. She's pretty, like a doll. That can talk. With no off switch.

It doesn't take long for the consoles to get switched on.

"Show me what you got?" Leandros points to an empty station. "I've been dying to play someone."

I wonder if any of the other under-eighteens have played *Cross Ups V* against anyone. We weren't supposed to tell people about the advance copies, but I bet I'm not the only one who broke that rule.

We pull our controllers out of our backpacks and

set up. This is it. Time for Jaden V to prove himself. No hesitation—I select Turan.

Leandros picks Kaigo. This should be interesting.

When the *FIGHT* sign flashes, we're standing in a circus tent. I jump over Leandros and go straight into my favorite combo, but he blocks before I can do much damage. I grab the trapeze to swing back over him and use the cross up to attack from behind. He goes down. But when I jump on him he bicycles me in the air—like we're one of the circus acts. Then he transforms into a dragon and spins sparkly smoke everywhere.

The sparkles are new, but that move was definitely Dragon Fire Super. What the heck? Is it just me who can't get it? As the rounds go on, Leandros pulls off Dragon Fire after Dragon Fire, like it's nothing. I'm so focused on figuring out how he's playing Kaigo, I hardly play Turan. I lose in two straight games.

"You sure about playing Turan already? I watched one of your matches from Underground Hype. You play a wicked Kaigo. I was hoping to play a mirror match with you."

I look at Leandros. He seems nice—like a big brother. I wish I could tell him the truth. But I'm

Jaden V now. I have an image to protect. "Yeah. I'm totally into Turan these days."

I glance around and see Kyle across the room watching Cali and Hena battle. "I'm gonna go check on Cali," I say and head over.

Hena's playing Goyle, the griffin-cross. He's a super-aggressive, arrogant guy. "I love the new graphics, don't you? The colors are so much more intense in *Five*, right? And the new settings are cool, but I wish we could pick where we fight. I like the changes to all the characters' clothing—more stylized, don't ya think? But Ylva's dress didn't need to get shorter, am I right? Why do they do that in video games?" Is she nervous, or does she always spew words like this?

One thing's for sure, she's good. On screen, her Goyle is keeping up with Cali's Ylva. She throws Cali to the ground and goes right into a Lion Roar Super. Since a griffin has the head of an eagle and the body of a lion, the roar sends sound waves out the beak, shaking the entire screen. Ylva twists around on the ground, taking the punishment.

Kyle nods toward Leandros. "Was that guy playing Turan already? That's nuts."

Watching from across the room, he must have

thought I was the Kaigo in our match up. Should I correct him? Jaden V says *no*. "He's just practicing her. I think he mains Kaigo."

"Oh. Doesn't want to give anything away before the tournament. Smart move, actually," Kyle says.

I hear a weird, muffled noise coming from the door. Someone in a huge yeti costume is waving his claws into the room. I look closer and realize it's Saki, from *Cross Ups*. The organizers must have ordered mascots for the launch. But why does it sound like he's calling my name?

The staffer at the door is refusing to let Saki in. So, this guy isn't part of the event? Must be some major fan.

A guy behind Saki is trying to get past the huge, furry costume. He's pleading his case with the staffer. As more of him emerges from behind the yeti, I see the guy is dressed like Kaigo. And it's not just any guy—it's Devesh.

He catches my eye and waves me over. I think of what Leandros and Gabe said. This is *so* not cool. By now the scene has got the attention of other people in the room. Cali's still mid-game with Hena, but anyone who isn't focused on a game is looking at the commotion.

What the hell? Do my friends think they can crash this party just because they're wearing *Cross Ups* costumes? Or because they know us? Jaden V can't be seen with them. I'll look like a loser. I shake my head and turn away.

A middle-aged guy wearing a white snapback *Cross Ups V* hat taps a microphone to get our attention. "Gentlemen," he says, and tipping his head toward Cali and Hena, "ladies. For those of you who don't know me, I'm Eddy Flaxsaw. I'm the brand-marketing manager at Marquee Games. I want to thank y'all for making the trip to New York this weekend to help us launch *Cross Ups Five*. We're real excited to have such a talented bunch of young players here show-casing our product. You've all had a chance to get a feel for the changes. Y'all like what we've done?"

A chorus of *yeah*s and general head nodding flows around the room.

"This afternoon we'll be on the main stage. I'm going to hype up the crowd, show them the trailer, and then you guys will battle it out. Y'all ready to play big and show off your best moves?"

I call out "Yeah," with everyone else, but my stomach does an air dash.

"We've chosen the best of the best. You're the players who will dominate *Cross Ups* in the coming years. Forget the OG. The time is right for the next generation—you!"

Gulp.

"And if playing the new game isn't exciting enough, how many of y'all are stoked about the chance to play Yuudai Sato?"

Louder cheers and head nodding. Even a few whistles.

"He couldn't be here this morning, but he'll be on stage this afternoon. And he's going to be watching y'all real close."

My thumbs get jittery and my stomach hurts, like Turan and Kaigo are sparring in there.

"Now, he's asked that you guys don't stop him and ask for autographs on stage. That would take away from your moment to shine. Instead, y'all can go to the meet and greet tomorrow. Get your autographs then, and ask him anything you want. And your speaker's badge will allow you to skip the line."

Meet Yuudai Sato? Ask him anything? I'm psyched, but only for a nanosecond. Will I even want to show my face to Yuudai Sato after I crash and burn in front of him at the tournament?

# CHAPTER 15

"Me and Gabe are gonna get some food. Wanna come?" Leandros says when the gathering ends.

"Sure." I speak before thinking. I have to meet my dad and Josh. Jaden V reminds me there's still a lot of time and it's no big deal if we eat before. "I'll get Cali."

"Let's keep it just us guys," Gabe says. "Girls suck the fun out of everything."

I consider, then decide Jaden V is cool and hangs with girls.

"I can't ditch Cali," I say.

Leandros's eyebrows go up. "Are you guys a thing?"

Why does everyone always think that? "It's not like that. She's my best friend."

"Friends with a girl? How does that even work?" Gabe says.

"He's only twelve. Remember?" Leandros says.

The comment stings, but I know these guys think Jaden V is cool. They asked me to come along, after all.

I head over to where Cali and Hena are talking. Well, really it's only Hena talking. I have to wait forever for a pause in the chatter. I talk fast. "We're getting food. Wanna come?"

Even though I'm clearly looking at Cali, Hena says, "Sure. I'm starving. I can literally eat all the time, how about you? My favorite food is pizza. I hope they have pizza. It's, like, the healthiest fast food, especially if you get lots of vegetables on it. Am I right? I like tomatoes and peppers but I don't like mushrooms. Did you know they're a fungus? Gross, right? But a lot of people still count them as vegetables . . ."

The five of us head down the long hall, following signs to the food court. Hena talks and talks. Gabe sighs and puts his earbuds in. So does Leandros. I pull mine out of my backpack and do the same. We roll our eyes at each other. Cali looks over and catches us.

The food court reminds me of the cantina scene from *Star Wars*, except the atmosphere is a lot friendlier. Creatures from all different worlds sit at tables chowing down next to regular humanoids.

Leandros heads to the burger place and we all follow.

When I pop out my earbuds I hear, "Aw, no pizza? I guess I'll get a burger too then. Hey, Jaden, when do you want to do our interview? Or would you rather stream a match together before you leave?"

"Um . . ."

"What are you talking about?" Gabe asks.

"Jaden's coming on my Twitch channel. I'm gonna help him get his video from T3 to explode," she explains.

"More like get your own channel to explode," Leandros grumbles. "Jaden, she's using you. I guarantee you'd be better off streaming some *Cross Ups Five* with me. I'll help you set up a better Twitch channel. Show you how to get more views."

"My videos get, like, three thousand views," Hena says.

"Three thousand?" Leandros laughs. Gabe joins in and they're loud, like they think she's so stupid. That's way more views than I've ever had, but Jaden V laughs along. Cali glares at me.

"That's nothing. You can't make money off that," Gabe says.

"Those are probably just guys who think you're hot," Leandros says.

"Whatever." Hena looks at me. "Cali said she'd come on my channel. You guys should really stick together. You're more marketable as a team."

"No way. Then they have to split the earnings," Gabe says. "That's not fair. He's a stronger player."

"As if. She beat him at Underground Hype."

"She's only been to one competition," Gabe says.

Cali looks like she's shooting Ylva's glittering lasers at him. "We all earned our spot here through rankings."

"Relax." Leandros pats Cali's head. "I'm sure you're a good player."

Cali squirms out from under his hand. Her own hands clench into fists.

"Whose channel do you want to go on, Jaden?" Gabe asks. "Leandros's or Hena's?"

His tone says I can't do both. Technically, I said yes to Hena first, but I didn't know I had options then. "Well . . . I've seen Leandros's stream before . . . ," I say.

"See? People actually know who I am," Leandros says.

Hena looks down, quiet for the first time since I met her.

"I'll go on yours," Cali says.

"Yeah, we can see who gets the most views," Gabe says.

Luckily, I'm up to order. I ask for a junior burger and don't get fries or a drink because the ten US dollars my dad gave me this morning, *just in case,* barely covers the burger.

It's so busy, there's no way we can find two tables together. No one bothers looking. Cali sits with Hena a few rows away from us.

It turns out Leandros is sixteen and Gabe is fifteen.

"You and Cali really should focus on getting a good following on Twitch. Or even YouTube," Leandros says.

Gabe says, "You're so young—that makes you stand out. If you wait until you're our age, there's way more competition."

I don't tell them Devesh streams our play on both those platforms. Our number of views is not going to impress them.

I wonder how Leandros got so popular. He and Gabe must be good players to be here, but so am I. They've both been to a lot of tournaments. Gabe tells us he even went to EVO last year.

"W—" I'm about to say *wow*, but catch myself. Jaden V is cooler than that. "What's EVO like?" I take a bite of my burger and lean back in my seat.

Gabe swallows, then wipes some ketchup off his chin. "Oh, man, it's so hype. You're up, like, 24-7. Playing all hours. You forget the time of day. The best players are there, just walking around with everyone else. You can end up playing some big names. I had a match up with a guy who beat Yuudai Sato the year before. I mean, he didn't win EVO or anything, but still, he had mad skills."

"How you stay up so long? You popping?" Leandros asks.

I'm confused. Popping?

Gabe smiles. "You know it. You too?"

Leandros smiles back. "Used to. My buddy had a prescription. But he moved. Can't get my hands on any."

They notice I'm lost.

"You have ADD?" Gabe asks.

"No," I say, offended. Does he think I have attention deficit whatever and that's why I don't understand what they're talking about?

"Too bad. There's drugs for ADD that help you calm down and focus," Gabe says.

"They work *real* good for gaming," Leandros adds.

Calm down and focus? I wish I could do that at tournaments. But taking drugs for it?

"They're harmless," Gabe says when he sees my expression. "Like, half my class at school takes them. I just borrow some for competitions." He pulls a pill bottle out of his pocket and puts it on the table.

Leandros slurps his coke through his straw, then says, "Everyone uses them. Even the pros."

"Especially the pros. They're not banned or anything." Gabe tosses his wrappers and napkins onto the tray. "Basically, if you don't, you're at a disadvantage."

"When I took one at Combo Breaker I was, like, totally relaxed, but also laser-focused the whole tournament," Leandros says.

I wonder if I could play Kaigo's Dragon Fire Super in *V* if I took one of those.

"I did better than I ever did before. Top sixteen," he adds.

"They're basically steroids for your brain. Here." Gabe shakes some orange-and-white pills into his hand.

"Thanks, man," Leandros says, taking one.

Gabe stretches his hand across the table to me. Turan hammers me from inside my chest. If I refuse, they'll think I'm a loser. I feel like I'm watching myself act out one of those cheesy say-no-to-drugs videos in health class. But is this the same? I mean, it's not *that* kind of drug. This one helps you.

I look around. We're surrounded by elves and trolls. Alice from Wonderland is sitting at the next

table. It's a crazy place. That must be why I do a crazy thing.

I take a pill.

I'll just put it in my pocket. They don't have to know if I actually swallow it, right?

"Now we're all even for the tournament," Gabe says.

"Might as well take it now." Leandros pops his hand to his mouth and takes a swig of his cola.

Gabe does the same, but first he tips his cup to Leandros. "Cheers!"

Good thing I didn't buy a drink.

Gabe notices and offers me his cup.

How do I play this cool? "It's okay – germs . . . I've got this thing on my lip." I bite my lip to hide the fact that there's nothing there.

"You can have the rest, I'm done."

I look down at the pill in my hand. What if it can really help me? Relax and focus—that's what I need to up my game. They said it's harmless. And it's not cheating if everyone takes it.

Suddenly Cali appears next to me with her tray. "We have to go."

# CHAPTER 16

As soon as we round the corner out of the food court Cali stops. I don't have to wonder if she saw what happened.

"What the hell was that?"

"The guys take this pill to help them play better. Don't worry, I wasn't really going to take it." *Was I? What would I have done if Cali hadn't shown up?*

"That's not what it looked like."

"Well, not everything is what it looks like."

"Is that why you look like Jaden but you're not acting like him?"

"What are you talking about?" But I know she means Jaden V.

When we get to the main entrance Dad and Josh are waiting for us with my costumed friends.

"You suck," Devesh says.

"That wasn't cool, dude," Hugh says. He's got Saki's head in his hands and he's dripping sweat.

Cali looks confused.

"Didn't you see us?" Hugh asks her.

"What are you talking about?" Josh asks.

Devesh tells them what happened at the door to the U-18 get-together.

I shrug. "What did you want me to do? You guys are so embarrassing."

"So, you're not going to wear your costumes tomorrow?" Devesh looks at me and Cali.

She shrugs. "You haven't even told us what they are."

"I got Ylva for you."

Cali wrinkles her nose. "I don't know . . ."

"But you play her all the time," Hugh says.

"It's just, she wears a dress." I've haven't seen Cali in a dress since she was little.

Devesh sighs.

"I'll look at it," she says. "Maybe, if it's not too short . . ."

"Well, I'm not doing cosplay. Real gamers would never." Leandros's words leave Jaden V's mouth.

"I went to a lot of trouble to get these costumes," Devesh says.

"You called your uncle," I say.

"My mom's cousin. All the way in India. You don't appreciate anything."

"No one asked you to get costumes. In fact, no one asked you to come here in the first place."

"Hold up now, boys," Dad says. "Sounds like we're all a little grumpy from a late night. Maybe a bite to eat will help. Let's get something to calm down the hangry."

We follow him out of the Javits Center. "There are food trucks out here," he says. "Half the price of food in that food court."

As we walk along, Cali fills everyone in on the U-18 get-together. I hang back, listening to make sure she doesn't say anything about the pill.

"How do fish tacos sound?" Dad asks. "Godlike?"

"We already ate. I'll just have iced tea." I stand back against the wall with Cali while everyone else lines up for food.

My stomach is churning and the smell of fried fish makes me want to gag. In less than two hours I'm going to humiliate myself on stage in front of a giant crowd of *Cross Ups* fans. This will be a million times worse than fainting in front of the whole school. Who knows how many people will be watching? One thing's for sure: Ty and Flash will be cheering for me to lose. And Hailey? What'll she think of me? My thumbs tap wildly. I shove them in my pockets and feel the bullet shape of the pill.

"Let's just wear the costumes tomorrow," Cali says.

"No," I grunt. "I really don't want to."

"It'll make them happy."

"Why should I care if they're happy? No one ever cares if I'm happy."

"Duh, they all came here especially for you. For us."

"Well, *I* never asked to come. Devesh asked my dad to bring us. I don't even want to be in this stupid tournament."

"What? You love *Cross Ups*."

"Yeah, well I don't love *Cross Ups Five*." *Because I suck at it.* Jaden V stops me before I say the rest.

"What are you talking about? We're going to meet Yuudai Sato," Cali says.

"I don't care. I wish we never came here." I need to stay angry so I don't start crying.

"You're acting like an idiot," Cali says.

Josh shows up with my iced tea. "That's because he *is* an idiot."

"Shut up."

"Just wear the stupid costume. Don't be a jerk."

Devesh emerges from the crowd with a soft taco in his hand. "Thanks, Josh. Does that mean you'll wear *your* costume this afternoon?"

"Sure," Josh says looking at me. "*I'll* be a team player."

# CHAPTER 17

"We're proud today to be launching the fifth installment of our *Cross Ups* franchise." Eddy Flaxsaw is on the main stage, which is a lot fancier than the one in our school gym and is lit by very warm, professional stage lights. Me, Cali, and the rest of the under-eighteens are sitting behind him in partners at the stations where we'll be playing. I'm next to Gabe, sweating.

I keep my eyes on the controller in my lap. The crowd here is a lot bigger than in our school gym. Even bigger than at either of the tournaments I've been to. And even though I don't have to talk, just sitting up here, facing all those people, makes my thumbs go crazy.

Eddy continues, the spotlight following him as he walks the length of the stage. "We're coming up to our twenty-fifth anniversary next year, and *Cross*

*Ups* continues to be one of the most popular fighting games on the market."

"Yeah it is," Devesh calls from the audience. He and Hugh are still in their costumes. They're standing with my dad, who's wearing Blaze's huge phoenix wings strapped over his *GDLK* T-shirt, and Josh, who's dressed like Goyle but looks more like some guy in a Shakespeare play. He's wearing a poofed-out green-velvet top with rhinestones over purple half-pants that lead to long stockings. The only thing he's missing is Goyle's heeled shoes. I hope no one finds out they're with me.

Eddy points to Devesh. "Right, Kaigo? We're confident that this latest edition is going to rock your world, and the gaming industry. So, without further ado, I present to you: the trailer for *Cross Ups Five.*"

The stage lights dim and the *Cross Ups* theme song plays as the screen lights up. I turn in my seat to see. As I rotate, I get a view behind the curtains. Someone's pacing around beside the stage, running his hands through his hair. Is that him? Yuudai Sato? It has to be. The audience is mesmerized by the special effects on the screen, but I can't take my eyes off my idol.

He's right there, like ten feet away from me. I could be breathing in the same air he just breathed out. Now he's biting his nails. I bite my nails sometimes.

The trailer ends and the crowd roars. When the lights come on, Yuudai Sato appears next to Eddy and the crowd screams louder. I scream on the inside, but real screaming—that wouldn't be cool.

"I think y'all know my friend, the *Cross Ups* god, the beast, the legend, Yuuuu-daiiii Saaa-tooooh." Eddy draws out his name like he's announcing a fighter for a boxing match.

"Hi, everyone," Yuudai Sato says into his mic. "What do you think of the new game?"

More screams.

I've never heard him talk before. I thought he'd have a Japanese accent, but his English is really good.

"We've assembled a phenomenal team of young players," Eddy says.

Yuudai Sato turns to us. "I hear you guys have mad skills."

"We think the best way to show y'all what *Cross Ups Five* looks like is through these young players who dominate the *Cross Ups* scene. And to lure them all here, we set up a sweet prize. Tomorrow,

on this very stage, the winner of today's tournament will play the best *Cross Ups* player in the world!"

"They will?" Yuudai Sato fakes confusion.

"I'm talking about you, Yuudai," Eddy says.

"Awesome, I can't wait!"

"Let's get this madness underway. Players, it's time to showcase *Cross Ups Five*."

The console screens light up and we all turn around. At least with my back to the audience, I can pretend they're not there. It's when I have to look at all those people, and especially when I have to talk, that I freak out. Now, with the screen in front of me, I can focus on one single problem—not playing like a scrub.

As we're setting up, Yuudai Sato walks around wishing all us U-18s good luck. When he gets to me, I nod and say a squeaky, "Hi." Not exactly Jaden V, but at least I look him in the eyes. They're brown.

Gabe fist bumps Yuudai Sato and taps his two fingers in a peace sign, right by his heart. No words, just a nod. I wonder if he's just acting cool or if he's really that unimpressed by the mega-star. Then I remember—he took the pill. Maybe I could be like that too.

I touch the pocket where I shoved mine. I wish I had taken it. But there's no time now. I wonder if Yuudai Sato takes drugs to play so good. The guys said all the pros do it, and he's a pro.

We focus on the small screens in front of us, but the audience is watching the jumbotron. It's split up to show all eight matches at once.

Gabe selects Blaze. I select Turan. We're fighting on another planet. The sky is purple and the ground is rocky. When the FIGHT sign flashes, we both go for a cross up. Turan and Blaze crash into each other in the air. Back on the ground, my crouching light punches are met with the same. Is this guy reading my mind?

Maybe, because somehow he predicts my Mind Control Super. Before I even finish transforming, he's got me in a headlock, pointing my horn at the sky so the shock waves don't get him.

"That's the way, son! You've got this!" Dad yells from the audience. I've heard him yell the same thing at Josh's hockey games, except Josh is actually winning. Does he think I'm winning? Or does he just think this is as close as I'll ever get? Maybe he just wants to show me he believes in me, like that kid on his team who misses every shot.

Luckily, Turan has one advantage. I pull the stick back and smash the top three buttons with the side of my hand and she's gone. See if he can figure out what I'm doing now. This time my Mind Control Super hits him. He writhes around on the rocks until I reappear. But then it's only a second before he's flying over me, raining fiery feathers like darts. I'm K.O.

I imagine all the kids from school watching this match. Who would vote for me now? I look like a total newb, which I basically am. What made me think that one week of practicing Turan would be enough to compete with her? Hailey is going to realize she was wrong. I'm not cool or awesome or godlike. I'm just a loser.

The *FIGHT* sign flashes. Again, I only dominate when I'm invisible. And since that only lasts for three seconds at a time, the round is over fast. And so are the next two. I lose the match and any hopes of representing.

Unfortunately, the torture isn't over yet. We're playing a classic, double-elimination-style tournament. That means even after losing this match, I'm still alive—I just move down to the loser bracket. I have to lose another match before I'm eliminated.

I unplug and head to the side of the stage. We have to report to Eddy between matches so he can record results and tell us who we're playing next.

"Drinks are in the cooler." He points over behind the stage curtain where a bunch of adults are waiting. He's not letting anyone out by the consoles, except Yuudai Sato.

Kyle leaps at me when I put down my controller to open the cooler. "What the hell are you doing, Jaden? Why aren't you playing Kaigo?"

"Uh . . ." Jaden V opens a bottle of water and

chugs to buy time. "I can do better with Turan. That was just a bad match."

"We talked about that this morning. It's stupid to play a brand-new character at a tournament."

"I just thought . . ."

"Well, stop thinking. Next match play Kaigo."

"Okay." I feel like Kaigo when he's all crumpled up after taking a beat-down. I've seen him like that a lot lately. Everyone's going to see it when I get owned in the next match.

My brain searches for a way out. Maybe I can say there's something wrong with my controller—act all confused when I make a mistake. ArcadeStix will be angry if I make their product look bad, but I can save my reputation. Save Jaden V. This is going to be my last match wearing an ArcadeStix shirt anyway. No way they're going to want me representing them if I can't do Dragon Fire Super.

My thumbs drum the water bottle at sonic speed.

What if I say I'm sick? The kids back at school might believe I have some kind of serious disease and that's why I fainted on stage last week.

I look at the huge crowd. Giant Blaze wings flap wildly. Dad knows I'm not sick. What will he say if I don't even try? To him, that's probably worse than sucking. He's not expecting me to do well anyway.

I could tell Eddy about the guys taking drugs to play better, but I don't think he'd care. Like they said, there's no rule against taking drugs.

I put my hand in my pocket and rub the pill between my fingers.

What if?

The sounds of the tournament and the Comic Con crowd fade away as I imagine myself as Jaden V in the *Cross Ups V* universe.

*I raise the pill to my lips as the FIGHT sign flashes. Suddenly, Jaden IV appears out of nowhere and smacks it out of my hand. We both dive to the ground where we grapple like mixed martial arts fighters. It's hard to tell who's who. A punch to the head, a knee to the stomach. After rolling around for what seems like forever, I stand victorious with the pill.*

*"Don't do it!" Jaden IV grabs my ankle and pulls me back down before I can get the pill to my lips.*

"Everyone else does it." I lash back with an elbow to the nose. "It's my only chance."

Blood gushes from Jaden IV's nose, but he still manages to flip me and pin me by the shoulders. Red droplets land on my face. "You're better than that," he says.

"Am I?" I thrust my hips up and grab Jaden IV by the neck with my legs. We somersault across the ground until we're both exhausted and gasping for breath.


The pill is in my hand when I hear Eddy call my name.

# CHAPTER 18

I plug in and look over at Kyle. He's staring me down. I select Kaigo.

A voice stands out from the crowd. "Come on, son. Show him what you've got."

I don't turn around, but I can picture my dad in the crowd, his wings getting in everyone's way. Probably telling people I'm godlike.

Hena's already there. She's picked Goyle again. I hate that guy. He can fill his Super Meter by taunting his opponent. It's so annoying.

"I was hoping I'd get to play you or Cali. Everyone is asking me about your skills on my stream chat. Now I'll be able to answer their questions."

I take a deep breath. Please, let me play decent enough so people don't think I'm a total loser.

I press Start. Then I panic and back dash across

the parking lot we're battling in. Hena doesn't follow. She just jumps Goyle up on the hood of a car and taunts me with a yawn and a stretch.

The last guy I played who used Goyle was a total jerk. He would be trash talking right now about how I'm running away like a baby. But Hena's chatting like we're besties. "I love that they decided to do this tournament. It's so much more fun than just a demo, don't you think? When it counts, we play at a higher level."

She's going to talk the whole time, isn't she? It's hard enough to play without my Dragon Fire Super, and even harder when she's talking the whole time. She moves in and fakes me out with a few random kicks, then uses my face as a punching bag.

I run at her with my bread-and-butter combo, but she's faster, grabbing me and spinning me over her head. "Do you like any of the new characters?" she asks, all casual as she sends me thumping over six cars. I jump up, but smash right into a twenty-two-hit combo to the face. I don't feel like Jaden V anymore. More like Jaden I.

"I love Turan." She smashes me through a car window. "The invisibility factor is huge. I think that's gonna be a game changer. I've been playing her a lot."

On screen, Goyle looks at his watch, like he's bored. This would usually get me so mad. But right now, I just wish she'd shut up so I can focus. I take a run at her again, this time with fireballs spewing from my mouth. She blocks them all, jumps over me, and kicks me in the back, talking the whole time. "The thing is, I've gotten so used to Goyle, I'll miss the taunts. But there are a lot of things he can't do."

Really? It doesn't look like it. The sound waves of Goyle's Lion Roar Super send me convulsing off the screen.

"I saw you playing Turan before," she says, following me across parked cars. "That's ballsy. I'm nowhere near ready to play her at tournament level yet."

My Super Meter is full now, but I can't concentrate with all her talking. I go to throw a Dragon Breath Super, but I'm so distracted I pull back instead of forward—the input for Dragon Fire Super.

Idiot.

But wait!

Kaigo actually transforms. A tornado of sparkly gray smoke swirls across the screen, taking out Goyle and several cars too.

I did it! I made those stupid sparkles. How? After two weeks of trying everything, it just works like that?

This could change everything. Can I do it again?

"I really want to play Yuudai," she says. "Or should I call him Mr. Sato? He's like a mega-star. He deserves that kind of respect. But still, it's weird, right? To call someone in their twenties *Mister.*" Hena doesn't miss a punch while she talks. But now I don't either because now I have hope.

As soon as my Super Meter hits the go-line, I play Dragon Fire Super again and hold my breath.

I've never been so happy to see sparkles.

A calm takes over my body. I've got this. This is what playing *Cross Ups* used to feel like.

I jump up and kick a rapid-fire fourteen-hit combo to her head. She misses a grab and I finally get a chance to throw her. She lands next to a burning car.

I glance at the meters under our feet. Hena hasn't got that much more Health than I do. Whoever gets their Super Meter full first will take this battle. I stay close and keep her busy with jabs and kicks so she can't taunt me. I send a fireball to explode the car behind her. It bursts into flames.

"Or should I call him by his gamertag? That would be weird, right? Maybe I'll just try not to use his name. Sometimes that's best."

I keep my eye on our Super Meters. Whose will be full first?

It's mine! Swirling sparkles are everywhere and she's K.O.

I jump up and punch the air!

I hear Devesh's voice over the roar of the crowd. "Yeah, Jaden!"

Jaden V is back in this! With my Dragon Fire Super I can totally do this. I'm on fire for the next rounds. I fight with everything I've got now that I've actually got a chance to play Yuudai Sato live.

In the next round, Hena starts out with another taunt. Goyle flicks his fingers to wave me over, like he's saying, *C'mon, show me what you've got.* The move leaves her open to attacks, so Hena's basically saying she doesn't even have to defend herself against me. A few minutes ago, being taunted like this would have broken me. I'd have been so humiliated, I'm sure I would have lost every round. But now that Dragon Fire is working, my confidence is through the roof.

If she wants to leave herself open like that, I'm going to take her down. Hard.

This time my bread-and-butter combo brings her to her knees. I pick her up and juggle her, then launch her into the nearest car window. She clambers out and aims her Lion Roar Super my way, but I duck behind a Bugatti and don't take any damage.

A few fireballs followed by a Dragon Tail Super that swipes her over the fence and she's K.O.

I feel my smile stretching across my face like the Joker's. Now I hope Hailey and the rest of Layton *are* watching. I'm finally representing.

Hena never stops talking and, now that I've got my Super back, it's actually kind of relaxing listening to her ramble on and on.

When the last *K.O.* pops onto the screen, I jump out of my seat. "Yeah! That's what I'm talking about!" I even do a little victory dance. Maybe it's not as cool as I think, but that's how happy I am that my best Super is working again.

At the side of the stage, Cali's waiting. "Jaden, I—"

"Just a sec," I say. Leandros and Gabe have hands up and I don't want to leave them hanging. I walk over to them.

"Nice," Leandros says as we high-five. "Finally someone took that girl down."

"She was trying to play mind games with me. You should've heard her," I say.

"Girls do that," Gabe says. "Talk, talk, talk while you're trying to play."

"You put her in her place. Way to represent," Leandros says.

"You see those guys in the audience going nuts?" Gabe asks.

"It's those same guys in Saki and Kaigo costumes who tried to crash the meet-up before," Leandros adds. "They were losing their minds when you started winning."

I don't know what to say, but I can't have these guys finding out how geeky my friends are. I roll my eyes and use Leandros's line again. "Real gamers would never, right?"

We laugh.

I catch Cali's eye. She's just a few feet away, hugging her controller to her chest. I bet she's listening in. It's hard to be Jaden V when Jaden IV's best friend is always around.

# CHAPTER 19

Everything goes right in my next matches because Kaigo and me are like one again. I wield his flames like a Jedi master wields a light saber. All those nights of struggling to make Dragon Fire Super work—were those just nightmares? Now I hit it every time. And easy too, like it's nothing. I actually have a perfect game against this guy named Andre from Boston in the last round. Can the pill be working from my pocket?

I'm glad I didn't take it, because it turns out I didn't need the thing anyway.

I look into the crowd. Devesh and Hugh are jumping up and down. My dad is clapping so hard it makes his Blaze wings flap. Even Josh is smiling.

Jaden IV wants to run over and celebrate with his crew. But Jaden V throws an arm in the air in a victory salute and heads over to Eddy.

"Working on a comeback, I see," he says.

"Oh yeah. It's on." I puff out my chest.

"Your next match is against Leandros," he says.

Looks like Leandros will get that mirror match he wanted.

-<o>-

"I'm playing a rising star of *Cross Ups*, twelve-year-old JStar," Leandros says. "This morning I decimated him during our practice session."

Why is he talking like that?

On screen, we're in the middle of a deserted street in some Old West town. A dust devil swirls in the background as Leandros's blue Kaigo approaches my red one.

"Thanks to all my fans who donated to help me get to this awesome event." Now I see the flashing red light on the console. He's got his phone propped up in front of us. He could have at least told me he's streaming to his Twitch channel.

Whatever. This kind of thing would have freaked out Jaden IV, but Jaden V is cool. After all, I did tell him I'd play on his channel.

I input my favorite combo. My Kaigo crouches, gives blue Kaigo two supersonic jabs, then leaps up and crashes an elbow on his head. Blue Kaigo shakes his head, spraying blood.

"Looks like the little guy has a move after all," Leandros says. "Two crouching light punches and Dragon Claw? Good choice. That's what I tell my friends to use when they're starting out."

Whoa, whoa! *When they're starting out?* I go for my favorite combo again, but he's ready this time. "Not so fast. You're not getting me with the same move twice. That only works with your grade-eight friends."

He throws me and I'm on the ground, then he is, then we both are, rolling along the dusty street until we crash into a covered wagon. I use this opening to unleash the sparkly tornado of smoke on him.

"Ooh, big move for the little guy. I can do that too," Leandros says as his Kaigo sparkles up the screen. Then the Kaigos roll around the ground some more.

"So, that girl you came with is pretty. You ever do anything besides play video games with her?"

Ugh. He's going there? On his live-stream?

I need to ignore him. His trash talk is just mind games. And I can play games too. I back dash down the street to a spot where some horses are tied up at a drinking trough.

"Why you backing away? Scared?" he says, following me along the dusty road.

Yes! He's taking the bait. When we get to the horses, I use them to launch myself up and over him so I can rain fireballs on his head. His Health Meter drops. It only takes one more Dragon Fire Super to knock him out.

"Yes!"

"JStar is lucky he got some help before this match," Leandros says.

Oh my god. Is he going to announce that Gabe gave us pills?

"I'm a bit of a mentor to this kid. I told him to play Kaigo, and he listened."

Maybe he thinks that's true.

He keeps talking through the match, about how cool he is and how much he's been "helping" me. I tune him out. Just like Hena.

Luckily, I paid close attention to his game play when we practiced together. He likes to play the ground and his bread-and-butter is swipe kick, uppercut. I spend a lot of time in the air, coming at him with huge leaps that keep me out of his kick range and make it easy to block uppercuts.

He loses the first three rounds. Now he takes the trash talk to the next level. "JStar here is into girl power. I found a nice little video out there of him on stage in a *Girls Rule* T-shirt. It's epic. Seriously, I'll post it later. He's standing there and then his eyes roll back in his head and he hits the ground like a . . ." He throws me and I bounce along in the dirt. "Actually, kinda like that. Totally faints. What happened there, Jaden?"

His Super Meter fills up, and I jump into a flying side kick, jabbing him in the throat before he can transform. Who's hitting the ground now? He lands at the saloon entrance and his smoke comes out in a sad little puff.

K.O.

He picks up his phone and brings it close to his face. "And that's it for this tournament. But I'll be streaming again later tonight. Keep an eye out." He taps his phone to stop streaming, then sticks out his hand. "Good game, man. Never should have given you that pill. And sorry about the words. Gotta keep up my persona, you know? My fans like it when I talk trash."

I guess that makes sense. And really, I don't care, because I'm crushing it. Jaden V is going to the finals.

"You're playing incredible," Cali says when I get to the side of the stage. Then she steps closer and lowers her voice. "Like, hard-to-believe incredible."

"I know, right? It's like my connection to Kaigo finally came back."

She tips her head to the side. "Seriously?"

"Yeah. And if I can play like that," I whisper, "like I used to—I actually have a chance."

She grabs me by the side of my T-shirt and pulls me back behind a divider where we're out of sight. "Jaden, we're best friends, right?"

"Yeah."

Eddy calls my name.

"So, we don't lie to each other, right?"

"Yeah," I say, more hesitantly.

"Tell me the truth. Why are you playing so good all of a sudden?"

Now Eddy calls Cali's name and we hear Kyle grumble. "They were just here."

"It's not what you think. I didn't take it," I say to Cali.

Her look says she's not buying it.

"Trust me, okay?"

"How am I supposed to trust you? You're acting like somebody else. You keep ignoring me."

Ugh, just because I hung out with Gabe and Leandros she's acting like I totally ditched her. "We don't have to spend every minute together, you know."

"I don't want to spend every minute with you," she says. "But best friends don't keep secrets from each other."

"There's no secret. I didn't take it!" I want to pull the stupid thing from my pocket and show her, but Kyle's found us now and he's striding in our direction. And anyways, why should I have to prove it to her? Best friends should believe each other.

"You could have told me."

"I just did. And anyways, I don't have to tell you everything."

Kyle's here now. "Don't you hear us calling you?"

"Um . . . sorry. What's up?" I say, trying to sound chill.

"Are you kidding me? The finals are about to start."

"Right. Let's do this," I say. *One more win and I'm playing Yuudai Sato tomorrow.* "Who am I playing?"

Kyle looks at Cali. "You didn't tell him?"

She smirks. "We don't have to tell each other everything. Right, Jaden?"

# CHAPTER 20

Eddy ushers Cali to the other side of the stage for what he calls a *dramatic entrance*. If only he knew the drama we've got going on.

There's a lot of action as the stage crew clears the stage so there's only one console left in the center, with a spotlight focused on it.

I stand next to Kyle, trying to listen to what he's saying. ". . . best-case scenario . . . ArcadeStix versus ArcadeStix . . . great for the brand . . ."

But all I can think about is how mad I am at Cali. Who does she think she is? She's always following me around, checking up on me like some kind of spy. And then she doesn't even tell me she made the finals. Now who's acting different?

The *Cross Ups* theme music starts and the stage lights go all swirly, like at the start of *Who Wants to Be a Millionaire*.

Kyle says, "Play Kaigo," and nudges me onto the stage.

The lights are dizzying. I can't look at the audience, and I don't want to look at Cali coming from the other side, so I just lock onto the two chairs set up in the center. When we get there, I want to sit down so I don't have to see the crowd, but Cali stays standing, facing everyone, so I wait, eyes on the chair back.

Even though I'm fighting to keep them still, my thumbs ricochet off the sides of my jeans. I look down and take deep breaths. *Keep it together. Jaden V does not faint.*

Eddy's on the mic. "We're down to the final two. Who would've thought they'd be our two youngest players? Jaden Stiles and Cali Chen are only twelve years old. I've been told they're actually next-door neighbors and best friends. All the way from Canada. Let's see how they battle up north."

The lights dim and we finally sit down. The jumbotron isn't divided into smaller screens anymore. It's showing our match in mega-size.

I focus on the small screen in front of us. I tell myself, *We're sitting at home on the couch. I usually win at home.* Then reality talks. *But not in Cross Ups V.*

I turn to Cali. She's the only thing standing between me and a match with Yuudai Sato. She knows how much he means to me. He's *my* idol, not hers. She could let me have this. But even if we weren't arguing, Cali's a hard-core competitor—she would never let up. I respect that.

We're both laser-focused on the small screen. I can actually feel the tension between us like the shock waves that come out of Turan's horn in the Mind Control Super. Can the audience sense it too?

Jaden V remembers gamer manners and sticks his hand out to offer a fist bump. It's shaking. Cali rolls her eyes and hits Play while my hand is still in the air. *Oooh*s from the crowd show me they've caught on.

She goes into an air dash before my hand is even on my controller and gets maximum damage off a twenty-three-kick combo because I can't block in time.

Cheap.

We're battling in an abandoned schoolyard at dusk. As soon as I'm out of hit-stun, I dive roll over the hopscotch game to get away. Then I immediately change directions, coming back at her with a flying kick she blocks easily. I panic and throw two crouching light punches and Dragon Claw, but Cali's expecting my go-to combo. She snorts and counters with a grab that ends in a massive body slam. My Super Meter is full now, but I can't use it because she's driving an infinite attack of punches into my head.

K.O.

Cali plays better when she's angry. This is not good for me. Even though I'm mad, I decide a peace offering is a good idea. For my sake.

I lean over and say, "I swear, I never took that pill. I can show you. It's still in my pocket."

She glares at me and angry-whispers. "Ugh, I believe you. Don't you dare pull that thing out now. People will think we both do drugs."

"You're not acting like you believe me."

"You're so jittery, there's no way you took that thing. Hena says it's supposed to calm you down."

"Ugh, you told Hena?"

"I just asked her what she knows about them. I never mentioned you. And anyways, you should listen to her instead of being so rude. I've learned a lot from her. Like, I know why you're playing so much better all of a sudden."

"What? Why?" I stare at her.

She hits the Play button and the *FIGHT* sign flashes again.

Unlike Cali, I don't play better when I'm mad.

Round two is a disaster. I throw fireballs everywhere, but none of them hit her. I'm K.O. way too fast.

I'm mad enough to shoot actual fireballs at her. She knows something about my *Cross Ups V* play and she's not telling me.

That's not cool.

"What do you mean you know why I'm playing better?"

"If you weren't being such a fraud, you'd know too."

Fraud? So, she doesn't like Jaden V. Well, she's going to have to get used to him. "Just because I'm more confident now doesn't make me a fraud. This is the new, improved me."

"Improved? You're so full of crap. You remind me more of Ty and Flash than Jaden."

Ouch. She's stooping low, comparing me to those jerks. "Whatever. You're the one who's hiding *Cross Ups* secrets from me to win the match." That's way worse than acting cool.

I'm so angry I can't focus. Ylva jumps around Kaigo like she's playing hopscotch. I look like a confused newb. It doesn't take long before I'm face down on the number-one square.

Jaden V needs to make a comeback, fast. If I lose another round this match is over. I turn to Cali, "Just tell me. I thought we were best friends."

"I don't want to be friends with someone two-faced like you. I heard what you said to Leandros and Gabe."

"What?" I totally stood up for Cali every time they trash-talked girls. "I never said anything bad about you."

"When they were talking about our friends. You acted like you don't even know them."

I knew she was listening in. It's like she's always there, wherever I go. I wish she'd just leave me alone. "*Our* friends? Hugh and Devesh are *my* friends. Get your own friends. Get a life."

## CHAPTER 21

As soon as the words are out of my mouth, I hear it.

I do sound like Ty and Flash. Or worse.

That's the meanest thing I've ever said to Cali.

Or anyone.

In my whole life.

Is Jaden V just a video-game-playing version of those morons?

Cali punches me in the gut. I don't fight back. It just seems wrong to hit her after what I said.

The last round is a total blur. Not because the characters are moving so fast I can't see the moves, but because things look blurry when your eyes are watery.

She doesn't care that I'm not fighting back. She unleashes an infinite attack that lasts until I'm K.O.

I rub my eyes on the shoulder of my T-shirt, hoping it looks like I'm rubbing sweat off my face.

People probably think I'm crying because I lost the match. They don't know it's way worse than that—I just lost my best friend.

I can't bring myself to look at Cali.

Next thing I know, there's a hand in front of me. "Good game."

It's Yuudai Sato lying to me. This is not how things were supposed to go. Jaden V was supposed to win. This was supposed to be the best moment of my life. I should be thinking, *I'll never wash this hand again.* Instead, I'm so embarrassed, I wish I could disappear like Turan. I want to forget today ever happened.

Yuudai Sato shakes Cali's hand too and says, "Congratulations, Cali. I'll see you back on this stage tomorrow."

Eddy raises her hand in the air. She doesn't look like she's been crying. "Congratulations to our winner, twelve-year-old Cali Chen, from Canada."

Cali heads straight over to Kyle at the side of the stage. I don't want to talk to either of them right now. I shove my controller into my backpack, slink into the crowd of other gamers, and follow Leandros and Gabe down the stage steps. I'm happy when they head in the opposite direction of Kaigo, Saki,

Blaze, and Goyle. I don't need them figuring out that's my crew. Plus, I really don't want to listen to my dad pretending he's so proud of me even though I lost. Again.

We cruise the exhibit hall. Leandros and Gabe are really hyper, talking nonstop. It's like walking around with two Henas. Are they acting like this because of the pills? I wonder if Hena takes ADD medicine too.

"Look at that." Gabe points at a table of *Cross Ups* action figures. "They have the new Kaigo already. How is that possible? The game's not even out—"

Leandros talks right over him. "How much are they? I want Blaze. We should all get our mains. Jaden, would you get Kaigo or Turan?"

Good question. The action figures are awesome. But I don't have any money. I bet my dad would get me one—if I was willing to be seen with him. I wonder why Leandros and Gabe think these toys are cool, but costumes are lame.

Suddenly I feel a tug on my arm. It's Josh. In his Goyle outfit. Ugh.

"We need to talk," he says.

"I'm busy."

"Who's this?" Gabe asks.

"I'm Jaden's brother," Josh says. He's older and taller than Leandros and Gabe.

"Nice to meet you, man," Gabe says, shaking hands. "Jaden's an awesome kid."

Now he's calling me kid?

"Cool costume. We should get costumes like our mains," Leandros says. I'm not sure if he's being sarcastic or if he really likes cosplay now. "You play *Cross Ups*?"

"Yeah, sure," Josh says. "Listen, I've got to talk to Jaden now."

"Go away," I say.

Josh leans down and talks into my ear. "Look, I don't want to drag you out of here, but I will."

I sigh and follow him. "Catch you guys later," I call over my shoulder. They're busy with the *Cross Ups* action figures again.

Josh leads me out of the exhibit hall and back to the entrance foyer with its glass walls and ceiling. It's not as bright anymore because the sun is starting to set. And since things are closing down soon, it's a lot emptier too. My friends are near the exit doors. Hugh is taking pictures of Devesh in his Kaigo uniform doing karate moves on Cali. The Saki head is on the ground next to them and Hugh's

hair is in wet ringlets. Josh leads me in the opposite direction.

"Okay, I tried talking to you nicely before. But now I'm pissed," Josh says.

Did Cali tell him what I said to her?

"Those guys over there"—he motions to my friends—"they're weird as hell, but they're one hundred percent on your team."

Wait, so this isn't about Cali? It's about the guys and the stupid costumes again? "Team? Maybe you didn't notice, but I play by myself. *Cross Ups* isn't soccer, where your team helps you win. When I lose, it's all on me."

"Fine, then they're the best cheerleaders you could ask for."

"Why does everything have to be about sports with you? You always have to remind me I've never been on a team. You just want to rub it in my face that I suck!"

"What? I'm saying you've got good friends and you're treating them like crap. None of my friends would ever do stuff like this. Hugh's been sweating all day because he dressed up like the freakin' Abominable Snowman for you."

"It's a yeti."

"Same thing." He sighs. "And you're not just dissing your friends. You're ignoring me and Dad. We drove all the way here for you and this is how you thank us? By acting like a rock star?"

"Whatever. Dad takes you to tournaments all the time. Don't act like you're always thanking him."

"Well, I don't totally *ignore* him. Stop acting like you're so cool."

"I'm cooler than you." We both know this isn't true. I remember his yearbook photos. Even at my age he looked cool. And it wasn't an act.

"You know what would be cool? Show some appreciation for your crew. Or else."

"Or else what?"

"Or else I'm telling Dad your new friends are on drugs."

What!? "Did Cali tell you?"

"Lucky guess. Man, Jaden, don't hang out with losers like that."

I roll my eyes.

"Seriously. You're better than that."

Dad comes out of the exhibit hall and heads toward us.

"We have a deal?" Josh says.

"Fine."

## CHAPTER 22

"Here," Devesh says, thursting a large paper grocery bag at me. "Wear it. Don't wear it. Whatever."

We're at the coat check picking up all the guys' stuff. He gives Cali a bag too.

I peek inside mine and see a bunch of snake heads. It's a Cantu costume. She's the hydra-cross from my dream. When she Supers, her neck divides into nine serpent heads.

Josh glares at me.

"Thank you," I say.

Josh clears his throat.

"It was nice of you to get these costumes," I add.

"He was going to give you Kaigo," Hugh says, "but this one's a better fit for you now, dude." Then, in case I didn't get what he's saying, he adds, "Because you're acting like you've got more than one face."

I've seen Hugh mad a lot, but this is the first time his anger's ever been directed at me.

"See you tomorrow," Devesh says, and the guys walk to the exit.

"I invited them for pizza," Dad says, "but Devesh said he wants to spend some time with his aunt."

I'm pretty sure they just don't want to spend time with me.

Josh looks at me and then at Dad.

"Thanks, Dad," I say. "And thanks for bringing us here."

The four of us grab pizza and bring it back to the hotel room. Bad idea. The only place to sit is the beds. We watch TV. No one says anything about Comic Con or the tournament or how I've been acting. Somehow, that means I can't think about anything else.

Finally, Dad says, "Jaden, come with me. I want to go check out the gym."

I consider telling him to take Josh instead, but something about the way he says it tells me this isn't optional. Plus, I don't want to be alone with Cali. She hasn't said a word to me since the stage.

Once we're halfway to the elevator, he says, "Son, I'm a bit disappointed . . ."

Well, it's official. Everyone hates me, including my own father. I'm nothing but a huge disappointment to him. "I messed up, all right. I should have played Kaigo from the start. That's why I didn't win."

"What?" He stops in front of the elevator but doesn't press the button. "I don't care about that. I just wanted to have a fun weekend with you."

I sigh. "You never actually thought I could win, did you?"

"That's not what I said, Jaden. You're twisting my words. What's going on with you?"

I watch the numbers light up above the elevator, showing it passing our floor. "I never even wanted to come here."

I reach for the button but he blocks me with his hand. "What do you mean? You asked me to bring you."

"Actually, it was Devesh who asked you."

"I'm confused. I thought this was a dream come true for you. You just met that Sato guy and played your favorite game."

"*Cross Ups Four* is my favorite game. Not *Cross Ups Five*."

"Okay . . . isn't it the same thing?"

"Ugh, you don't understand. I was good at *Four,* but I suck at *Five,*" I say.

"Suck? You just made the finals. Why would you say you suck?"

"I couldn't do my Dragon Fire Super. Well, now I can again, but I wasted all this time practicing Turan in training mode and then . . . I didn't win."

"I'm not too sure what you just said." Dad chuckles.

"Basically, it means I'm not like Josh. He wins everything and I'm just a big loser."

"Is that what this is about? You and your brother are very different. But you have to know, there's no winner or loser in a family. You're brothers."

"Yeah, well, I wish I didn't have a brother. Everyone thinks I suck compared to him."

"Well, from what I saw, your game play was top caliber. It's your attitude that *sucks,* as you say." He uses his fingers to make quotation marks in the air when he says the word *sucks.*

"Whatever."

"Didn't you see all those people cheering for you today? Look, being different from Josh isn't a bad thing." He pushes the down button. "I don't want you to be Josh, son. But you aren't being *you,* either. *That's* what worries me."

◄O►

In the morning, I'm the last to get a turn in the shower. I put on my jeans and the red ArcadeStix shirt. When I come back into the room Josh is dressed as Goyle again. The way he's prancing around the room, I think he actually likes the outfit. Dad's wearing almost all the Blaze gear, including a feathered hoodie that looks like a phoenix head with the beak coming off his forehead. The only thing he doesn't have on is the wings—they're too big for this room. Even Cali is wearing the Ylva cavewoman dress over black leggings and her red shirt.

They all look at me. Josh shakes his head, but no one says anything. As we head out the door, Dad grabs his wings and the shopping bag with snake heads hanging out. "Just in case you change your mind."

Funny thing is, if we'd had these costumes last year at Halloween, at the start of grade seven, I'd have thought they were awesome. I'd have fought Devesh for the right to wear Kaigo, but I would definitely have gone trick-or-treating wearing any one of these. Even Goyle. Me and my friends would have had a blast. And the year before that, in grade six, I probably would have thought it was funny if Dad surprised me wearing that Blaze costume. I'd have rolled my eyes, but I'd have been okay with it.

Next year I'll be in high school. I can't be dressing up with my dad. Don't Devesh and Hugh get that?

When we get to the Javits Center, I want to ditch them, but I can't because of my deal with Josh. There's already a long line to see Yuudai Sato. We find Saki and Kaigo near the end.

"Cali! You look amazing!" Devesh says. He probably thinks that every day.

Hugh looks at me. "Seriously, dude?"

I shrug.

He shakes his head.

"Why aren't you guys at the front of the line?" Cali asks. "I thought you were going to get here super-early."

Devesh hangs his head. "We got on the wrong ferry. Ended up at the other side of town."

Hugh smiles. "It was kind of cool though. We saw the Statue of Liberty."

"By the time we got here it was ten after ten." Devesh sighs.

"All these people lined up in the first ten minutes?" Dad says, looking down the huge line.

"It's Yuudai Sato," we all say together.

Dad walks toward the front of the line, counting the people in front of my friends.

"Why don't you guys take our badges and use them to skip the line?" Cali says. "We already met him."

I glance at my badge. I can't believe she's offering to give away my one-on-one talk with my idol. I spent all night planning questions to ask him. She gets to talk to him on stage later. But this is my last chance to say something to him without sounding stupid.

Devesh brightens, then deflates. "That won't work. Which one of us looks like Cali Chen? Plus, won't Yuudai Sato recognize you guys?"

"Hugh could wear his Saki head." Josh says. "No one will know if there's a guy or a girl under there."

"What if they check? We could get kicked out. And we'd lose your passes," Hugh says.

"True," I say, trying not to look too relieved. "How would we explain that to Kyle? Sorry guys." I feel bad as we leave them behind and head to the front of the line.

# CHAPTER 23

We show the volunteer our badges and he walks Cali and me right up to Yuudai Sato.

"Ah, my friends from the finals yesterday," Yuudai Sato says. "You still talking after that battle?"

We lie.

"You ready?" he asks Cali.

"Yes, sir. It'll be an honor to play you."

"The honor is all mine," he says. "I cannot rest on my previous record. I have to show each game that I'm still a worthy opponent."

I don't know how long we have, so I blurt out my first question. "How do you decide which character to play?" Yuudai Sato is known for playing three different characters. Blaze, Cantu, and Kaigo.

"Ah, yes. You played Turan yesterday. Then Kaigo." He puts his hand on my shoulder. Yuudai Sato's hand—the hand that controls his game play—

is touching my shoulder. "You know, the characters tell me who to play in each game."

I stare at him. Then say, "Do you think I should keep playing Kaigo or switch to Turan?"

"You know what creature Turan is?" he asks.

"She's a luduan," I say.

"Yes. You know about luduan? You're Chinese, right?"

"Yeah, my mom's Chinese. I just know luduan is like a deer with a unicorn horn."

He laughs. "True. But luduan also has many powers. She can travel incredibly fast around the world and she speaks every language."

"Cool," I say.

"Most important, luduan is a detector of truth. She knows what is real and what is fake."

"Oh," I say, fingering the pill that's still in my pocket from yesterday. What would she think of this?

"What do you know about dragons?" He's asking me more questions than I'm asking him.

"Dragons? Different cultures have different kinds of dragons. They're always long and snakey. They've got scales and claws. Some have wings, but not Kaigo. He's an eastern dragon. Or maybe he's a drake—

that's a kind of dragon without wings. Also, young Western dragons don't have wings until they get older, so there's a chance he'll grow wings later, but I don't think so. All dragons can breathe fire—"

He cuts me off. "You know a lot more about Kaigo."

"Yeah. I've been playing Kaigo a long time."

"Yes. Your connection is strong. I see that."

Ha! So I'm not crazy. The guys always laugh at me when I say I have a special connection to Kaigo.

"Such a connection takes time. You need time to get to know the characters, just like friends." He gestures to Cali.

He's right. I can tell you everything about Cali,

Devesh, and Hugh. What do I really know about Leandros and Gabe?

Cali changed characters. She used to main Saki, but now she mains Ylva. But she played Ylva in secret for a long time. By the time Cali used her at Underground Hype, she was really connected to the dire wolf–cross. Cali dominates with Ylva now. I hope one day I can play Turan like that.

Problem is, if Turan is a truth detective, she probably doesn't like Jaden V.

I'm about to ask my next question when the volunteer calls, "Time's up. Next."

"Thanks, sir," I say.

I can't believe I just got advice from the best *Cross Ups* player in the universe.

But wait, I forgot to ask him to sign my controller.

◄O►

Kyle's standing with Dad and Josh when we leave Yuudai Sato.

"Can I have a minute with these guys?" he asks.

"Sure, we'll go get a spot near the stage," Dad says, gesturing to the main hall entrance.

I'm still freaking out that Yuudai Sato knows who I am when Kyle steers us to a bench to sit. "That was an incredible showing yesterday, you guys," he says. "You're blowing up on social media right now and ArcadeStix couldn't be happier."

We smile. I hope he can't tell that we're totally not talking to each other. Well, really, it's only Cali who's not talking to me because she's mad. The only reason I'm not talking is because I don't know what to say to fix things. I suck at saying the right thing. I don't want to make things worse.

"Cali, your game play was really on point. You made some smart choices in your matches."

"Thanks," she says, smiling.

Kyle turns to me. "Let's talk strategy, Jaden."

I knew this was coming. My high from talking to Yuudai Sato deflates. Is he going to kick me off the team? Yuudai Sato might never hear of me again.

"If you had played Kaigo from the start, you wouldn't have ended up in the losers' bracket. You could've won this thing. No offense, Cali."

She shrugs.

I look down. I guess I can tell him the truth now, since I redeemed myself. "Sorry, it's just, I was having trouble with Kaigo, so I thought I could do better with Turan."

"What do you mean you were having trouble with Kaigo?"

"I don't know. When I played at home I couldn't get Kaigo to do Dragon Fire Super. But then something happened and I could do it yesterday. I guess my connection to Kaigo came back when I was competing."

"Wait a second. Did you download the patch?"

"What patch?"

"Didn't you read the instructions that came with the game? There were some glitches in the advance copies. Kaigo's Dragon Fire was one of them. You were supposed to go to the game store and download a free patch. There was a code."

I think back to that first day, ripping open the box in my living room. I thought I didn't need instructions.

"Why didn't you say something?" Kyle asks.

"I don't know." But I do know. I was too afraid to admit I was having trouble. If I had been honest and told Kyle, or anyone, I wouldn't have wasted all that time freaking out. I would have been playing a perfect Kaigo from the beginning. I probably would have won.

I look at Cali.

"You knew."

"Hena mentioned it yesterday."

"And you didn't tell me."

"You were there. She was talking about it on the way to lunch."

That's what Cali meant when she said I would know if I wasn't being such a fraud.

Jaden V didn't hear Hena because he had his earbuds in to drown her out.

I'm standing with Josh and Dad near the stage waiting for the match to start. The truth is, there's a small part of me that hoped Cali would give me her spot to play Yuudai Sato, since he's my idol and everything. But I guess, even if she offered, I'd have to say no. I mean, everyone watched me lose to her. It would look pathetic if I took her prize.

It's ten to twelve when Hugh and Devesh find us. Their faces are droopy.

"What's wrong, boys?" Dad asks.

"They closed the line before we got to the front. Yuudai Sato had to leave so he wouldn't be late for the match," Hugh says.

"This has been the worst weekend ever," Devesh says.

Dad goes into cheerleader mode. "Don't say that. We've had a lot of fun this weekend. Right, Jaden?"

"Yeah, for sure. Um, New York City, right? . . . I have to go to the washroom," I say to get out of range of Josh's laser glare. I feel bad that the guys didn't get to talk to Yuudai Sato. But it's not my fault.

When I walk into the men's room, there's a heaving sound coming from one of the stalls. Gross. Someone's barfing.

As I'm washing my hands, Hugh comes in carrying the paper shopping bag.

"Dude, you *need* to wear this."

"I don't want to."

"C'mon. It'll make Devesh feel better."

"Look, real gamers don't wear costumes. You think Yuudai Sato would wear that?"

"I know you think you're a superstar now, but I hate to break it to you—you're no Yuudai Sato."

The stall door opens and Yuudai Sato walks out.

# CHAPTER 24

Our mouths drop open. I want to run into one of the stalls and hide.

He goes to the sink, cups some water and brings it to his mouth. He's the guy who was barfing? Maybe he didn't hear what we were saying.

"Are you okay?" I ask.

He looks up and sees my reflection in the mirror. His eyes glance down at my ArcadeStix T-shirt and back up at my face. "Oh, yeah." He glances back at the stall. "Sorry about that. Gross, right?"

"You want us to get someone for you or something?" Hugh asks. "They have a first aid station."

"Nah, I'm good. Happens every time I have to go on stage."

"Oh, like pre-game jitters? Lots of athletes do that. Like that soccer player, Messi. He threw up on the field all the time." *Shut up, Jaden.* I'm rambling random facts I heard from Josh.

"They don't call it e-sports for nothing," Yuudai Sato says, ripping some paper towel from the dispenser. "So, what do you think I won't wear? That Saki costume?"

My cheeks heat up like Kaigo's fireball.

"Our friend bought us these *Cross Ups* costumes. He's really bummed because Jaden won't wear his." Hugh pulls a few snake heads out of the bag.

"Cantu? Nice. Personally, I'd go with Kaigo. Or Ylva, if I had the legs for it. But I have to wear this." He points to his *Cross Ups V* shirt.

"But real gamers don't do cosplay, right?" I say, straightening up. Maybe when Hugh hears it from Yuudai Sato, he'll finally get why I can't be seen in that thing.

Yuudai Sato tosses the wet paper towel in the garbage and shrugs. "If you can play, you're a real gamer. It has nothing to do with what you wear. Just be you."

"Whoever that is," Hugh mumbles.

My shoulders sink.

Yuudai Sato is heading out the washroom door when I have an idea. "Wait. Mr. Sato, sir, I know you're in a rush, but can I ask you a quick favor?"

As we head out of the washroom, I stop and throw the pill in the trash. Yuudai Sato said I should be me. That's not Jaden V. And anyway, being cool is a lot of work. It's way easier being Jaden IV.

But first, I'm being Cantu. I've got almost the full gear on, and it's pretty detailed. The black tunic has golden, Greek-pottery-style embroidery around the hem and neck. Eight black snake heads attach around my neck like a scarf. My head is supposed to be the ninth snake head. I guess I can't argue with that. I skipped the golden bracelets and headband. I have my limits.

"Devesh is going to be so happy," Hugh says from inside his Saki head. He's bouncing along next to me clapping. "I knew you weren't too cool."

I take that as a compliment.

The heads stretch out from my shoulders, bumping people as I walk. For the second time in my life, I'm wearing girl clothes. Luckily, most people are focused on the bubbly yeti skipping along at my side. At least I won't be on stage today, so no one back home will see me like this.

We head back to the others just as the lights dim and the *Cross Ups* theme song starts to play. We're all in the first row with me at one end, followed by Hugh, Devesh, Josh, and Dad—the *Cross Ups* superhero team.

Devesh raises his eyebrows when he sees me. I smile my best this-is-fun smile and put up my hand for a high five. He rolls his eyes and looks back at the stage.

Eddy's hyping up *Cross Ups V* again. When he introduces Cali, the spotlight follows her as she walks across the stage in her Ylva dress, wearing a *Cross Ups* cap and waving to the crowd like a pro.

She's acting super-confident—and I don't see Josh lecturing her. I guess the difference is she's not faking it.

I hear some commotion and turn to see Leandros and Gabe pushing through the crowd. "Our friend is saving us spots up there," Gabe says.

"Nice costume." Gabe snickers, pushing aside a few of my Cantu necks to make room to stand.

My cheeks burn like Kaigo breathed fire on them. Jaden IV might not care about being cool, but these guys only know Jaden V.

"You see that guy in full-on Blaze gear?" Leandros asks when they get to me.

I shrug and feel my thumbs vibrating against the side of my leg.

"Yeah, yesterday he only had the wings, but today he's all in," Gabe says.

"He's an old guy too."

I flash back to me and my dad painting those droid costumes. We had to wear these masks when we were spraying the paint so we wouldn't breathe in the fumes, and he kept making these Darth Vader sounds and saying, "I am your father." We laughed so hard. I wonder what version of Jaden that was.

Was that the real me? All I know is everything was easier back then.

"You know what?" I say. "Maybe he's just being nice and dressing up for his kid."

"Maybe," Leandros says. "That would actually be cool. My dad would never do anything like that for me."

"My dad didn't even come watch me play yesterday. And we only live half an hour from here. Hey, is that your brother standing with Blaze?" I look down as Gabe makes the connection. "Oh my god. That's *your* dad."

# CHAPTER 25

My cover is blown. Jaden V is officially dead. No point pretending to be cool anymore.

The crowd cheers. I didn't even notice that Cali just won the first round.

I glance over at my dad again. Someone's stuck in his wings. It's Hena. Once she's free, she smooshes herself past the whole front row to stand in front of Leandros with her phone in her hand. "You are such a liar. Why would you say those things?"

Leandros raises his hands and eyebrows together.

"What are you talking about?" I ask.

"He called me boring. Said I never shut up. Told people not to go to my channel unless they want to 'test themselves to see if they can handle the torture of someone talking about the most boring things in the world.'" She reads the last part from her phone.

I look at Leandros, who gives a crooked smile. "C'mon. You talk a lot."

"Okay, maybe, but you didn't have to say I'm so boring and tell people not to go to my channel. That's just mean."

Leandros shrugs.

"You guys know what he says about you?" Hena asks Gabe and me. "Calls you 'losers.' Said, 'Gabe and Jaden use drugs to win.'"

Gabe shakes his head in disappointment. "Seriously? You took it too, bro."

Hena does a double take. "What? It's true? You guys gave drugs to a kid?"

"I never took it," I say. Leandros and Gabe raise their eyebrows, but I think Hena believes me.

"You guys are messed up," Hena says.

"He makes it sound like he's taught you everything you know: 'JStar was a falling star. Totally overrated. Until I came along and helped him out.' He even said Cali cheated to beat him."

I stare at Leandros. Maybe he thought I took the pill. And maybe I am overrated, but one thing's for sure, "There's no way Cali would cheat. How dare you say that."

"I was just talking smack. That's what my viewers like. You gotta give the audience what they want."

The crowd *ooohs*. Cali's taking serious damage on the big screen.

Leandros says, "I'll help you build a following and then you'll understand what I mean."

"Um, no thanks. I don't want your help," I say.

"Come on, I thought we were friends," Leandros says.

"So did I. But that's not how you treat friends." I look at Hugh and Devesh cheering for Cali. I wonder if they've heard any of this. I turn to Hena. "You know what? I will go on your channel. How about an interview after this match? We can set the record straight about Leandros."

She gives me a thumbs-up and a huge smile.

"Whatever. No one's going to see it," Leandros says as I push past Hugh and Devesh to stand between them and my dad and Josh.

"Hey!" Dad says, like he's still glad to see me after I totally ignored him all weekend.

We go nuts together for every hit Cali lands.

"I wish that was me up there," I say.

"Ah, next time," Dad says. I know there will never be a next time, but I smile anyway.

Cali doesn't win any more rounds, but she represents for ArcadeStix, and Canada. And for our crew.

At the end, Yuudai Sato takes the microphone and says, "Cali, thank you for a great game. I expect to see you at the top of many tournaments in the future."

The crowd applauds. Our crew cheers like crazy. Devesh *hoo-hoots* and Dad puts his fingers in his mouth and whistles really loud.

Yuudai Sato continues, "I want to call up a young man who waited in line to see me today. Devesh, please come on stage. I've heard good things about you, and I'd like to meet you right now."

Devesh's eyes bug out as he points to me. Then he screams and runs up on stage.

"These costumes you got for your friends are awesome," Yuudai Sato says.

"Meeting you is awesome!" Devesh screams into the microphone.

My fake smile has transformed into a real one. Devesh is never going to forget this moment. I hope it's enough to show him that I know who my real friends are.

"Sorry I missed you earlier. Is there anything you want to ask me?"

Devesh takes the microphone and starts talking to the crowd like he does this all the time. Like he's Ryan Seacrest or something. "Actually, I lined up for two reasons. First, to tell you that you're godlike . . ."

The crowd applauds this.

Devesh's voice gets louder ". . . and second, to ask you to tell the students of Jack Layton Senior Public School in Toronto to vote for my man, Jaden Stiles!"

He hands the mic back to Yuudai Sato. "All right, did you hear that kids? Vote for Jaden Stiles. Come on up here, Jaden."

There goes my plan of not being on stage. As I climb up, I realize I'm not freaking out. Maybe it's because all that time on stage for the tournament got me used to looking at a crowd from this angle.

Or maybe it's because this moment is just too much. It doesn't even feel real. My idol just did a live commercial for my election campaign.

Hailey is going to love this.

"That Cantu costume was a perfect fit," Hugh says. The two of us are wedged in the back seat this time. With all the backpacks stored at our feet, our knees are by our chins.

"Yeah, it was totally you," Devesh says.

"Ha, ha. I get it. I was acting two-faced."

"Actually, I mean you thought you were a goddess. But two-faced is good too."

I let them lay into me. It takes a while for them to really believe the old Jaden is back. Fortunately, it's a long ride.

Cali's a different story. She's sitting next to Devesh in the middle seats, but she's not talking to us, she's talking to my dad. At first, they're talking about the weekend, then about her mom and school. Cali's father lives in another city and he's not much of a dad. Not like my dad anyways. He'd never take her on a road trip like this. He's kind of only interested in himself.

Our car jets us north, through the darkest night. By the time we get home it's almost midnight again. None of us falls asleep this time.

—◦—

I'm lucky the next day is a holiday so there's no school. The election is Tuesday. I'll be really thankful when that's over.

I can't use the speech Devesh wrote. It's all lies. Everyone knows I didn't win the tournament. Or battle Yuudai Sato. And I obviously didn't beat him.

Does it even matter what I write for my speech? It's not like I'll be able to stay standing on that stage long enough to finish the first sentence.

And really, why should I bother? What do I know about being a vice president? Would I be any better at running the school than Ty and Flash?

I sit at my computer with a blinking curser in front of me but no words on the page.

For an hour.

There's no point. I can't deal with this speech problem when there's something way more important on my mind.

I get up and head downstairs.

# CHAPTER 26

I ring Cali's doorbell in my socks. We never bother putting on shoes to go across the porch. If this goes okay, then I can survive whatever happens at school tomorrow. I can live with losing the election. What I can't live with is losing my best friend.

When she answers I say, "I'm sorry. I was a jerk."

She raises her eyebrows.

"I didn't mean what I said. I like you always being around. It was just making it hard for me to act cool. But I've figured out I don't actually want to be cool."

"Well that's good, because you're probably the uncoolest person I know."

I wince. But I deserve that.

"I talked to Hena," she says. "She told me what you said to Leandros. *That* was cool."

I look down. "I never should have tried to be friends with him. You guys were right—he was totally using me."

"She also told me about the interview you did for her channel. I just finished watching it."

"Ugh. I've been so busy with my speech I haven't even seen it yet. I hope I don't look like too big of a geek."

"You totally look like a geek. But it's actually cool, because you're not acting all fake."

Cali agrees to help me, and we spend the rest of the day preparing a new election speech. By the time dinner's ready, I'm happy with what we've got. And more importantly, I've figured out a way to deliver it without passing out.

I select my clothes very carefully the next morning. No glitter, no sparkles, no *Girls Rule*. Even though Hailey thought that was cool, it's not really me.

The assembly is first thing in the morning again, so right after attendance, me, Hailey, Flash, and Ty go down to the gym. Madame Frechette has us sit in chairs in the first row. I wonder if Hailey talked to her about us not being on stage.

"Ready to fall on your face again?" Ty asks.

"For your information," Hailey says, "Jaden is totally ready to deliver his speech." I've let her in on my plan.

I feel everyone's eyes on me as they come in the gym. Sounds like they're all talking about me and Cali and Comic Con. But I don't get the feeling they're putting me down. In fact, some of them look impressed.

At the back of the gym I see my parents, sitting next to Ty's dad, who I recognize from the arena, and another woman who's not a teacher. Maybe Hailey or Flash's mom?

Once all the classes have arrived, Madame Frechette introduces us.

Hailey climbs onto the stage and takes the microphone. "Hi, Layton. I'm Hailey Williams. I'm running for student council president along with Jaden Stiles for VP. I spoke to you all last week about making this an amazing year full of memories. And we're totally serious. We really want everyone to have an awesome school year. Everyone.

"If we are elected, we promise to help you remember all the awesome things that happen at school. We're planning a digital yearbook. We'll compile video clips of all the fun stuff happening at Layton to show you at our weekly assemblies. Then, at the end of the year, you'll have a whole school year's worth of digital memories.

"And you can decide what memories matter. A good report card or making the basketball team aren't the only things that make you feel happy at school. So don't worry about being different. It would be so boring if we were all the same. Just be you and show us why you love coming to school. We'll add it to the digital yearbook!

"Jaden and I can help you all make memories this year. Whatever that means to you. Jaden's already started. Let's take a look."

I look over at Devesh. He double clicks the icon that says, "Memorable Moment #1" on his laptop. I wasn't sure he was going to help me with this. He insisted on watching the video first to make sure it was Jaden IV and not Jaden V on there.

I pop up on screen wearing the full Cantu costume, including the headband and bracelets this time.

"Good morning, Layton. Jaden Stiles here to ask for your vote. I know a lot of you are thinking, *Why should I vote for Jaden Stiles? He's supposed to be a rising star, but he didn't win that tournament.* The truth is, I'm not the best *Cross Ups* player.

"Yet.

"But I'm going to keep working hard and, one day, I will be.

"I'm also not the best vice president.

"Yet.

"But if you elect me, I promise I'll work hard to get better at that, too.

"You're probably thinking, *but that guy fainted saying three words in front of the school. How's he supposed to handle being VP?* Well, if I can go from falling on my face to giving a speech in front of the entire school in just ten days, imagine what I can do for our school in a whole year.

"You're probably also wondering why I'm dressed like a Greek goddess. I'm wearing this to show my friends I want to keep making awesome memories with them.

"This is actually my second memorable moment. In case you missed it, here's number one."

The video switches to the stage at Comic Con and Yuudai Sato looking into the camera. Devesh has edited him onto a loop and added a stutter so it goes, "Vote for Jaden Stiles. Vo-vo-vote for Jaden Stiles. You hear that kids? Vo-vo-vote for Jaden Stiles."

When the lights go on, I look over at my parents. Mom and Dad start clapping with everyone. Dad stands up halfway, then catches himself, looks over at me, and sits back down.

Hailey beams at me from the stage.

Suddenly, it feels really weird to be sitting on this chair while she's up there. Before I can think it over, I climb the stage steps and stand next to her.

Her smile stretches even wider as she grabs my hand and raises it to the sky. "Let's start making some memories together. Vote Jaden and Hailey."

Next Madame Frechette introduces Ty and Flash.

They bring a bunch of other people up on stage with them. Five girls wearing black leggings and matching red tank tops line up behind them. They all have their hair in a side ponytail. Two guys stand on either side of Ty and Flash. They're all wearing red Layton jerseys. Probably guys from the volleyball team.

Ty glances over at his father and gives a little cough to clear his throat.

Flash starts in on the beatbox rhythms. The volleyball players start to break-dance. The girl in the middle starts to move and the others follow, one beat behind.

Ty coughs again and begins.

*"We're Ty and Flash and we're here to say,*
*Vote for us, there's no other way.*
*We're . . ."*

There's a long pause, and then Ty says, "Can we start over?"

Madame Frechette nods.

Ty looks at his dad, who's shaking his head and chuckling.

Flash starts the beat again and the dancers join in.

Ty runs his hands through his long blond hair, coughs a couple of times and raps.

*"We're Ty and Flash and we're here to say,*
*Vote for us, there's no other way.*

*We're on all the teams, we know how to win,*
*You really want a school that's run by Jaden?"*

Flash does a *"wicka-wicka-woo"* sound and the dancers all go *"Oh!"*

Hailey looks at me and rolls her eyes.

*"We'll make this school dope, just wait and see.*
*Don't be a loser, don't vote for Hai—"*

One of the break-dancers kicks a leg up, knocking the mic out of Ty's hand. Everyone laughs as he scrambles across the stage to get it.

Madame Frechette says, "You know, boys, it's against the election rules to put down the opposing candidates. I think it's best if we stop you here."

Yes! This time they're the ones with an epic fail. And minutes before the vote, too.

Hailey dashes up onto the stage and leans over to speak into Flash's mic. "It's okay, Madame Frechette. We think Tyrell and Willard should have a chance to finish their presentation."

What is she doing? If they stop now, we're practically guaranteed a win.

Hailey looks over at Ty's father in the audience, then back at Madame Frechette. "They worked hard to prepare this song. They should get to present it."

And she's not being sarcastic either. It takes me a second to clue in.

She's brilliant. She just proved that she really wants *everyone* to make happy memories—even Ty and Flash.

"Do you think you can finish your song without insulting your opponents?" Madame Frechette asks Ty.

"Uh, yes, ma'am."

Ty and Flash and their crew start again. Of course, Ty can't do what he promised. He's got the rap memorized, and he can't change it up on the fly. Every time he gets to a part that disses us, he just says "yeah" instead of our names. He messes up a lot of lines, but doesn't ask to start again. I know how he's feeling. I've been there. He just wants to get off the stage as fast as he can.

When they're done, Madame Frechette goes over the process for voting again. We'll know who wins by the end of the day.

I head over to my parents.

"Sorry, son. Didn't mean to embarrass you," Dad says. "We'll leave now."

"No. I'm glad you came."

Mom smiles. "Your speech was great. But why didn't you say it live?"

Dad smiles. "Our son is very creative. I'm so impressed that you came up with a way to deal with your stage fright. I would've told you to imagine the audience in their underwear. But that never really works."

Next to us, Ty is hanging his head.

His dad says, "You had that at home. What happened? Don't tell me you got stage fright. You need to be more confident."

Wow. Maybe me and Ty aren't that different after all.

◄○►

I'm at my locker before last period when Madame Frechette's voice comes over the speakers. "Attention Layton students."

I freeze.

This is it.

I'm about to find out what the rest of my grade eight year is going to be like.

Over by the gym doors Ty and Flash are surrounded by a bunch of guys from their teams. They all look pumped, like they're ready to erupt in cheers at any second. But the wrinkle on Ty's forehead shows he's not totally confident this time.

"Excuse me," Hailey says, as she squishes past some students who actually stopped to listen to the announcement. Her locker's at the other end of the school. Only Hailey could get here in ten seconds. She's not even out of breath, but she *is* shaking with excitement when she grabs my hand.

"May I have your attention please?" Madame Frechette continues.

Um, no. Hailey is holding my hand.

"I have the results of today's student election here before me. I'm pleased to announce that your new president and vice president are Hailey Williams and Jaden Stiles . . ."

She's still talking but people are clapping and congratulating us so I can't hear the rest of her speech.

Hailey hugs me. I think I'm going to like this student council thing.

Devesh, Cali, and Tanaka come running at us, crushing us in hugs.

"My man!" Devesh says. "I knew you could win!"

We hear Hugh's squeal before we see him. His hug almost knocks me to the floor. "Dude!"

"C'mon." Hailey leads me past a lot of people with hands up for high fives. She's heading to the gym doors. Everyone in the crowd around Ty and Flash is shaking their heads and looking annoyed. What's she doing?

She sticks out her hand. "Well-played, guys," she says.

"You won, right?" Flash says, doubtfully shaking her hand.

"Yeah. I'm just congratulating you guys on a good race. You obviously care a lot about our school if you ran for office. I hope we can work together in the future to make this school even better."

Ty ignores her hand and puffs. "As if. We don't have to do any work. You're the president and VP. You do the work."

I bite my lip to keep from laughing. But I get where they're coming from. They have to act like they never even wanted to win. That's just how it works.

That's what I would have done if we had lost.

When we turn away from them we almost slam into Mr. Efram. "Way to go, you two. You'll do a great job."

"Thanks, Mr. Efram," Hailey says, shaking his outstretched hand. "We have a lot of plans for this year."

"I'm sure you do, Hailey," he says.

I reach out and shake his hand, too, surprised at how confident my grip feels.

He winks at me and says, "And you, JStar . . . you're like a whole new guy this year."

"Oh, no, sir. I'm still the same old Jaden." Sort of.

He looks like he doesn't believe me. "I guess I'm just seeing a different side of you."

I think of Kaigo's strong dragon side and Ylva's fierce dire wolf. What kind of Supers does a vice president have? I guess I'm about to find out.

# ACKNOWLEDGMENTS

The talented writers in my WIP critique group—Anne MacLachlan, Patrick Meade, Sandra Clarke, Heather Tucker, Karen Cole, and Steve Chatterton—have all helped to make Jaden a stronger character and to make me a better writer. Thank you.

Early drafts of this story were also read by Barbara Hunt, Cynthia Englert-Rattey, Bev Fiddler, Angela Dizes, Martin Siefarth, Brigitte Siefarth, and Adelyne Scheltema. Thank you all for your feedback. The story is better because of you.

The Writers' Community of Durham Region continues to be my main source of support and inspiration.

Special thanks to Jason Das for answering my infinite attack of questions about gaming systems and updates. I truly appreciate your patience and creative thinking.

Thank you to the team at Annick Press, especially Katie Hearn and Kaela Cadieux. Also, to the amazing illustrator, Connie Choi, whose artistic eye makes the Cross Ups books so visually appealing.

And most importantly, thank you to my incredibly supportive family. My parents helped with everything and my husband and kids are my biggest cheerleaders! I love you all.

Sylv Chiang is a middle grade teacher by day and a writer of middle grade fiction by night. She lives in Pickering, Ontario.

 Connie Choi graduated from the Bachelor of Illustration program at Sheridan College. She lives in Toronto, Ontario.

**BOOK 1**
**OF THE CROSS UPS SERIES**

Jaden knows he could be the best
at *Cross Ups*, the video game he can't
stop playing—if only he didn't have to
hide his gaming from his mom . . .

After an epic match leads to an invitation
to play in a top tournament, Jaden and his friends
Devesh and Hugh hatch a plan to get him there.
But they'll have to face
some serious obstacles along the way.